"Don't do this, T

"Don't do this? You ha... me after—" She stopped herself. She was seeing a side to Morgan she hadn't known existed. Maybe it was better this way, but it certainly wasn't the best timing.

He stuffed his hands into the pockets of his blue jeans. "I just want you to know that I still..." he began without looking at her. Slowly he raised his gaze to hers. "I still care about you, Trish, and that's why this is so hard. I don't want you to get the wrong idea, because I don't want you to be hurt."

Trish opened her mouth to tell him she'd already been hurt, possibly far more than he could guess, but he'd turned and walked away. She needed to tell him she was very likely pregnant, but he wasn't making it easy for her. Maybe for now, and until she was sure, she should say nothing.

Dear Reader,

One of my favorite movies is *Hope Floats*. In it, Justin Matisse (played by Harry Connick Jr.) tells young Bernice Pruitt, "I'll see you around. That's what's so great about a small town." Anyone living in or having visited a small town for any length of time knows this to be true, especially when it comes to that one person you hope to avoid. That's exactly what happens to Sheriff Morgan Rule when his former fiancée returns to Desperation, Oklahoma, after her children's book promotion tour. But was Trish Clayborne's tour the real reason he canceled their wedding and broke their engagement?

Our lives are a series of small and large events that affect us in many ways, whether we realize it or not. One event in Morgan's life not only caused him to make a major change, but also gave him a reason to reevaluate his life and offered him another chance at that happily-ever-after he longed to have.

I hope you enjoy Morgan and Trish's journey to the rediscovery of their love for each other and the changes their lives take on that journey. There'll be another Desperation, Oklahoma, story coming in 2011, introducing new characters and revisiting familiar ones. Enjoy love in Desperation!

Best wishes and happy reading!

Roxann

The Lawman's Little Surprise

ROXANN DELANEY

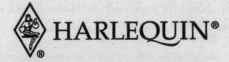

HARLEQUIN®

TORONTO • NEW YORK • LONDON
AMSTERDAM • PARIS • SYDNEY • HAMBURG
STOCKHOLM • ATHENS • TOKYO • MILAN • MADRID
PRAGUE • WARSAW • BUDAPEST • AUCKLAND

Recycling programs
for this product may
not exist in your area.

ISBN-13: 978-0-373-75317-8

THE LAWMAN'S LITTLE SURPRISE

www.eHarlequin.com

Printed in U.S.A.

ABOUT THE AUTHOR

Roxann Delaney doesn't remember a time when she wasn't reading or writing, and she always loved that touch of romance in both. A native Kansan, she has lived on a farm, in a small town, and has returned to live in the city where she was born. Her four daughters and grandchildren keep her busy when she isn't writing or designing Web sites. The 1999 Maggie Award winner is excited to be a part of Harlequin American Romance, and she loves to hear from readers. Contact her at roxann@roxanndelaney.com or visit her Web site, www.roxanndelaney.com.

Books by Roxann Delaney

HARLEQUIN AMERICAN ROMANCE

1194—FAMILY BY DESIGN
1269—THE RODEO RIDER
1292—BACHELOR COWBOY

Don't miss any of our special offers. Write to us at the following address for information on our newest releases.

Harlequin Reader Service
U.S.: 3010 Walden Ave., P.O. Box 1325, Buffalo, NY 14269
Canadian: P.O. Box 609, Fort Erie, Ont. L2A 5X3

Tons of hugs and thanks to
Kristi Gold and Kathie DeNosky,
the bestest brainstorming buddies a writer
could have, even when it means getting no sleep.
And a special thank-you to those who serve in
law enforcement and risk their lives to keep us all safe.

Chapter One

Trish Clayborne sat in the warmth of her car at the stop sign, blinking away the tears filling her eyes. *Home.* She was almost home.

From the intersection of the county road and the main street of town, Desperation, Oklahoma, resembled something out of a foggy dream. Colorful, twinkling lights draped the storefronts, and giant red-and-white candy canes adorned each of the streetlights. A misty haze, caused by the remnant of the dusting of snow that barely covered the ground, created halos around the lights and gave the deserted street an eeriness that contradicted the friendliness of the town and its inhabitants.

Trish had grown to love Desperation and everyone in it after she and her sister, Kate, had arrived to live with their father's sister eleven years earlier. Aunt Aggie had quickly filled the void left by the death of their parents in a tornado, and the people had accepted them with open arms. The sisters had both thrived and become a part of the community. It was home, and Trish was grateful to be back after having been gone for six weeks on a book promotion tour that had seemed to last forever.

It wasn't until the flashing lights of a sheriff's cruiser filled the interior of her car that she realized she had been sitting at the intersection for more than several minutes. Dread filled every fiber of her being. The last man she wanted to see was probably behind the wheel of the cruiser.

The sheriff approached, casting a shadow into the car. Slowly, wishing she could disappear, Trish pushed the button to roll down her window. But instead of greeting the sheriff with a smile, she continued to stare at the misty scene before her, hoping the knitted cap she wore would hide her blond hair and her identity until she could stop her heart from racing.

"Having car trouble, miss?"

She turned slowly, wishing she could be anyplace but where she was.

"You're back," Morgan Rule said, his voice flat and matter-of-fact.

She tried her best to ignore his frown and the lack of emotion in his voice. "You knew I'd be home before Kate's wedding and Christmas."

"The wedding is a week away. You could have stayed and done some sightseeing."

She bit the inside of her cheek to keep the tears at bay. Not long ago, this man had loved her, had wanted to marry her. They'd planned a future together. But something had happened to change him. He wasn't a man who wore his emotions on his sleeve, but somewhere, sometime he had forgotten how to smile and apparently to love.

"Whose car is this?" he asked, stepping back and taking it all in with one long look.

"Mine. I bought it with money from the sale of my book." Money she had planned to spend on their wedding.

His dark eyebrows shot up as he turned his attention back to her. "I thought you couldn't drive."

"I've known how to drive since high school, I just never did. You know that."

"Yeah, maybe I do. Maybe I forgot. Easy to do when you're not around to remind me."

"Out of sight, out of mind?" she asked, and instantly wished she hadn't.

"Something like that."

He hadn't been out of *her* mind. Not for a minute. And now that they were alone, with no one to hear, maybe they could find a way to work things out. "Can we call a truce, Morgan? For the holidays, if nothing else."

"A truce? Are you saying you want to be friends? Is that it?"

She nodded, hoping to somehow regain what they had lost when she left. He was a good man, kind and gentle, a serious man who cared deeply for others, but rarely let it show. If only she could find that man who'd changed six months ago.

Placing his hands on the window opening, he leaned down, his dark gaze connecting with hers. "Our wedding was canceled. You had other things to do. I don't see a reason to be friends."

"I *postponed* our wedding," she pointed out, while attempting to remain calm. "You were the one who canceled it."

A flicker of emotion crossed his face, something she couldn't recognize, and was gone. His eyes betrayed nothing.

Without thinking, she laid her gloved hand on his. "Now that the tour is finished—"

"What's done is done." Pulling his hand away, he avoided looking at her.

She had hoped he would be more reasonable than he'd been six weeks ago, and it was breaking her heart that he hadn't changed. "But it doesn't have to be that way."

Taking a step back, he focused on her, his gaze intent. "When are you leaving again?"

The question caught her off guard. It was clear the subject of a truce and rediscovering at least their friendship if not their love was closed. "I don't know that I am," she answered.

His nod was short and curt. "To make this easier on both of us, here's what we do. I'll avoid you and you avoid me. There's no reason to get everyone in town talking—and you know they will, no matter what—so let's just be civil when we do run into each other."

Civil? Was this his idea of being civil? She didn't know what had happened back in June, but whatever it was, it had changed him. And she didn't like this man he had become.

Knowing that arguing would be useless, she shrugged her shoulders and stared out the windshield at the lights. "If that's the way you want it."

"It is."

Her heart ached, but she wouldn't let him see how much she was hurting. "Then I'd better be getting home. Aunt Aggie and Kate are probably wondering where I am."

When he didn't respond, she slipped the gearshift into Drive, looked both ways and proceeded slowly across the street, headed for the Clayborne farm a few miles beyond town. Temptation drew her gaze to the rearview mirror as she rolled up her window, and she could see Morgan standing in the street where she'd left him. He wasn't watching her, just staring at the spot where she'd been. Stuffing his hands into the pockets of his jacket, he turned for the cruiser, its lights fading away behind her, adding to the eerie glow of the night.

With a sigh, she tried to focus on the road ahead, but her mind was on what needed to be done and just how she would do it. She had thought when she'd sold the children's book she'd written that life would be rosy. She'd been engaged to a wonderful and well-respected man, and they'd been planning their upcoming wedding.

And then her publisher had offered her the chance to promote her book with a book-signing tour. As far as she was concerned, it was a one-time thing, not something she planned to do again, and she had been excited, even though it meant taking a leave of absence from teaching her second-grade class. Morgan had instantly hated the idea and had threatened to cancel the wedding. The night before she left on the tour, after they'd made love, he'd announced that the engagement was off and he was canceling the wedding. She'd begged him to reconsider. When he wouldn't, she'd insisted that he at least tell her why, but he'd refused to give an explanation. She still didn't know the reason.

And now she needed him more than ever, but she hadn't decided how she would tell him the news she had. Not with him still feeling the way he had six weeks ago when she'd left town.

IT HAD TAKEN every bit of control Sheriff Morgan Rule had to keep from going after Trish and retracting everything he'd said to her. But he wouldn't do it. Not now, not ever.

He'd been so proud of her when her children's book had been bought by a well-known publisher, and he'd thought he'd finally found peace and happiness. He should have known better. Instead of peace, one incident with the town drunk had brought back the memories he'd thought he'd buried and reminded him that he could never have a life like most men. He hadn't meant to hurt Trish, but to save her. And now, because he didn't trust his heart, he had to say and do things he knew were hurtful—to both of them.

Morgan mounted the stone steps of what had once been a Southern mansion built in the wilds of Oklahoma long before it was populated. He opened the front door, hoping to slip quietly up the stairs to his apartment. He was lucky to live there, thanks to his uncle who managed the place. But luck had vanished when he'd realized the car he had stopped was Trish's. His uncle met him inside the front hallway of the Shadydrive Retirement Home, affectionately nicknamed the Commune by its residents.

"I thought I heard your car," Ernie Dolan said, hurrying around the corner from the large dining room. "Everybody's still at dinner, so if you're hungry, you can—" He stepped closer to study Morgan, his blue eyes revealing his concern. "Something wrong?"

Morgan shook his head, and then let out a long sigh. He might as well say it. Everyone would know soon enough. "Trish is back."

"She is?" A smile broke out on Ernie's face, but he quickly raised a hand to his short, graying beard, covering his chin to hide the grin. "I mean, how do you know?"

"I stopped to check out a car—"

"Did I hear someone say Trish is back?"

Morgan turned to see the newest of the residents closing the doors to the dining room behind her.

So much for quiet solitude in my apartment.

Hettie Lambert hurried toward them, her gray eyes sparkling with excitement. "She's back? Is she at Aggie's? Oh, it will be so wonderful to see her again and hear all the news about her tour."

Thinking of the blue Eclipse Trish had been driving, Morgan grunted. "There should be plenty of that, considering her new car."

Hettie clapped her hands together. "A new car! Good for her. She's been at the mercy of everyone else's schedule far too long."

Morgan didn't necessarily agree, but he kept his opinion to himself. He liked and admired Hettie, deferring to her sixty-plus years on most things. But they had butted heads over his cancellation of the wedding, and she still wasn't ready to accept that it was over between Trish and him.

Hettie nearly always held the winning hand, but she did it with her usual grace. The citizens of Desperation thought highly of her, and there was no reason not to. And although she would say it wasn't true, she was the matriarch of the town.

She had donated the Ravenel mansion, which had been built by her great-great-grandfather, Colonel George Ravenel, in the late 1800s, for use as the Shadydrive Retirement Home. It had been Ernie's idea to provide a place for those who no longer wanted the upkeep of a house, whether in their golden years or before. It was a grand addition to the small community, and the waiting list to acquire one of the seven apartments was long.

"Did the two of you get a chance to talk?" she asked, her voice lowered as if in a conspiracy.

"Yeah, we talked," he muttered.

"That bad, huh?" she asked. Sighing, she slowly shook her head. "Stubborn male pride."

Morgan pressed his lips together and said nothing, knowing that if he kept quiet, Hettie would give up. She loved an argument, even on those rare occasions when she didn't win. If he refused to talk, she would drop the subject—at least for a while—and that's all he needed for now.

"There'll be other times for the two of you to talk," she said with a smile and turned for the stairs. "Plenty of time during the holidays. I'll just give Aggie a call and find out the latest scoop on Trish's travels and how the tour went."

He watched as she continued up the stairs, fending off the dull ache he'd been feeling since he realized he couldn't go through with the wedding.

"Go on and get a bite to eat," Ernie said, turning back to Morgan when Hettie was gone.

"I'm not hungry," Morgan replied, and started for the stairs.

But his uncle stopped him. "Don't be hard on Hettie. She loves you both and wants to see you happy."

Morgan could only nod as a large lump formed in his throat. He'd told Ernie what had happened to his partner in Miami six years ago, but he had never told Hettie and never intended to. Nobody needed to know about it.

"It's Christmas, son," Ernie said, breaking into Morgan's thoughts. "A time of forgiveness."

Unwilling to discuss his problems, Morgan shrugged his shoulders as he continued up the stairs. "So they say."

He hadn't been in his tiny apartment on the third floor more than twenty minutes when someone knocked on the door. Kicking the boots he had removed out of the way, he went to see who would want to bother him. He wasn't in the mood for company.

Hettie stood smiling on the other side when he opened the door. "I have a favor to ask," she said.

Feeling guilty that he'd treated her badly earlier, he opened the door wider. "You know I'm always happy to help."

"You've always been a dear."

"So what is it?" he asked, not sure what the twinkle in her eyes meant and not sure he really wanted to know. But he'd committed himself, so backing out wasn't an option.

"You know how I hate bad weather. We've never had much snow here, and I hate to drive after dark."

A muscle twitched in his jaw. He had a feeling he wasn't going to like this favor. "What little snow there is out there wouldn't give you any trouble."

"That may be true, but these old eyes aren't what they once were, if they ever were," she said with a smile. "Especially after dark. So would you mind taking me out to Aggie's?"

He knew exactly what she was doing. "The matchmaking has to stop, Hettie. I can take care of myself."

"Of course you can," she said with a wave of her

hand, the silver bracelets on her thin arm clattering. "Besides, there's no match to make. It was made long ago."

"Hettie—"

"And I already told Aggie I was coming."

"Ernie can take you."

"No, he's busy. Either you take me or I don't go, and I dearly want to see Trish."

But Morgan didn't. In a town as small as Desperation, avoiding someone was nearly impossible. It would be hard enough to see her in town again, where they would surely run into each other. Hadn't he finally come to the point where he had stopped expecting to see her around every corner? To hear her voice, her laughter, when he least expected it?

When he didn't reply, Hettie continued. "You don't have to talk to her. I know for a fact that Dusty is there. You two men get on well with each other, so you can just ignore us chatty females and have a nice visit of your own. I promise not to stay late."

He doubted it would be that easy, but he wouldn't deny Hettie her visit with Trish, no matter how much he didn't want to see her again. "All right," he conceded, "but just this once."

"HE'S JUST STUBBORN," Trish's sister said as they sat at the big kitchen table. "Heaven knows most men are, at one time or another. Maybe I could have Dusty work on him and—"

Trish nearly shot out of her chair. "No, Kate! Please don't say anything to Dusty." She calmed the panic that her sister's remark caused and tried for a smile. "I'll work it out."

Kate shrugged. "Whatever you say, but one of these days, Morgan Rule is going to regret all this."

Trish wondered if that was true. She had always admired Morgan's dedication to his job and the way he enjoyed helping people. But now that she'd felt the effects of how stubborn and unreasonable he could be, her heart felt bruised and battered.

From the kitchen sink, Agatha Clayborne gave an unladylike snort. "Pride goeth before the fall, and it's been pretty telling around here that when Morgan broke it off with you, there were plenty who thought it was wrong. Why, just yesterday when I stopped in at the post office to mail that package, Betty asked how you were doing. And I told her—" She looked toward the door at the sound of a car pulling up the drive. Wiping her hands on a towel, she smiled. "There's Hettie, I'm sure. Trish, you get the door for her. There's only one reason she would be here and that would be to see you."

"And you," Trish added as she stood and caught the look that passed between Kate and Aunt Aggie. Perplexed, she walked to the door and opened it. There was only one person who knew she was home and told Hettie, and that would be Morgan. Hearing the sound of more than one car door closing, she looked outside and saw the cruiser under the glow of the yard light. Two people were approaching the house, one a tall, regal woman, the other wearing a Western-style law enforcement hat and not at all in a hurry.

Morgan had driven Hettie out to see her. Should she be pleased?

Before Trish could answer her own question or even begin to calm the flutter in her stomach, Hettie hurried up the steps and around the porch to the kitchen door to wrap her arms around her.

"I was worried the weather might cause you problems," Hettie said. "I see you made it home, safe and sound."

Smothered in Hettie's warmth, Trish was still aware of Morgan mounting the porch steps. "The roads are fine, Hettie," she assured her aunt's best friend. "I didn't have any trouble at all." At least not until she'd made it into Desperation, but she wouldn't say so with Morgan so near. "Come on inside," she said when Hettie released her. Glancing at Morgan now standing behind Hettie, she included him in the invitation. "Both of you. Aunt Aggie has coffee and some of Kate's famous cinnamon rolls from this morning."

"Now I'm glad I skipped dessert," Hettie said, laughing, and entered the house. Trish followed when Morgan took the door and held it for her. A nod to him was her thank-you. It was the *civil* thing to do.

Kate rose from her chair to be wrapped in Hettie's arms, as Trish had been, while Aunt Aggie placed an extra cup of coffee on the table. "Evening, Hettie," Aggie said, and then turned to the sheriff who stood silently by the door. "Morgan, Dusty's in the living room watching a football game or something on television. I'm sure he won't mind the company. There's a cup of coffee for you there by the sink. Kate or Trish will bring the rolls in a few minutes."

Trish watched Morgan fidget with his hat and thank her aunt. He also avoided looking Trish's way as he picked up the steaming mug from the counter and disappeared into the hallway.

An uncomfortable silence filled the room, until

Aggie moved to the table. "Sit down and take a load off, Hettie," she said as she settled on her favorite chair. "You, too, girls."

Hettie took a seat to the left of Aggie and turned to look at Trish. "Is that fancy new car I saw when we pulled up yours?"

Trish finished her sip of coffee and put her cup down, thinking of Morgan's earlier remark about her car. "When I ordered it, I asked to have it delivered to one of the dealerships in Oklahoma City so it would be there when my flight arrived today."

"The snow tonight was quite a surprise. It wasn't any problem for you?"

"None at all," Trish answered. "It barely covers the ground, and it's been warm enough that the highways and roads are clear. But it really wouldn't have mattered. I had a lot of practice driving in the snow with rental cars in Chicago."

"Chicago! At this time of year, that must have been a real experience."

Trish laughed, remembering her first time driving in snow. Sliding into a snowbank taller than the hood of the car hadn't been her idea of fun. "I learned the hard way."

Hettie leaned back in her chair, as if checking for sounds from the living room. Leaning forward again, she lowered her voice. "Morgan seemed a bit put out about that car."

Glancing at the doorway behind Hettie that led down the hall to the living room, Trish shook her head and sighed. "He acted as if I had no right to be behind the wheel of any car."

Beside her, Kate reached over and patted her hand.

"Be patient with him. He isn't accustomed to you being so independent. Personally, I'm so proud of you, I could bust, but he's obviously in a state of shock over it."

"Could be he's just been missing you and didn't want to admit it," Hettie added.

"Who's been missing who?"

All four women sat up straight and did their best to look innocent. Kate jumped to her feet, a big smile on her face, and hurried over to her husband-to-be. Linking her arm with his, she said, "Why, Dusty, I'm missing you."

He grinned at them, obviously not believing Kate. "If you say so, hon. I just came in to find out where those cinnamon rolls are. Morgan and I are wasting away in there."

"Yes, you are so wasting away," Kate said, pinching his side and laughing.

"I'll get the rolls." Trish hurried to the cabinet. She envied her sister. Had it been only a few months since she and Morgan had teased each other the same way? It seemed like years. Now they were working to be civil.

Forcing a smile, Trish took a plate piled high with rolls to Dusty and hoped he didn't see how disappointed she was. After all, she still had some pride.

"Any messages?" Dusty asked when she handed him the plate.

She looked up at him. "What?"

"Messages. You know. For him." He jerked his head in the direction of the living room.

Shaking her head, she managed a real smile. "No, no messages."

He turned to leave, but stopped to lean down and whisper to her, "Hang in there."

It was apparent that Kate had kept him updated on the latest happenings, and Trish felt a small rush of embarrassment. But she quickly reminded herself that her sister—and her sister's fiancé, too—cared about her and didn't like to see her hurting.

When Dusty had taken the snacks to the living room, Trish returned to her seat at the table, hoping the conversation could turn to anything other than her problems or even her trip home. She didn't want Morgan to overhear anything that might be said about him.

She needn't have worried. Hettie asked about Kate's wedding gown, and before long, the upcoming wedding on Saturday was the main topic. Trish quickly forgot that Morgan was anywhere nearby as she joined the discussion of the pros and cons of an outdoor wedding in mid-December.

When Hettie announced it was long past time to leave and that Morgan was probably checking his watch, reality returned.

"I need to get a magazine I meant to show Kate earlier, before I forget," Trish said, excusing herself. "I'll stop by to see you sometime this week, Hettie. With all the things still left to do with Kate's wedding, we'll be in town nearly every day, I'm sure."

"Of course you will," Hettie said. "The committee meeting for the New Year's Eve party is Thursday at the Commune."

Great, Trish thought. One more place where she'd risk seeing Morgan. "I'd completely forgotten about that," she admitted, "but I'll be there."

After giving Hettie a quick goodbye hug, she escaped and hurried upstairs to her bedroom. Grabbing the magazine she had tossed to her bed earlier, she started down the stairs, listening for sounds of Hettie and Morgan's leaving. When all seemed quiet, she reached the bottom and turned to walk down the dark hall. But she let out a squeal when she nearly collided with a tall, solid man.

"Sorry," Morgan said, reaching out to steady her, and then pulled back immediately. "I didn't mean to scare you."

Catching her breath, she calmed her pounding heart with her hand. "Well, you did." They stood there for a moment, the light from the kitchen barely reaching them. It unnerved her, and she finally broke the silence. "Why are you still here?" she asked, keeping her voice as quiet as possible. "I thought you'd left with Hettie."

"She wasn't ready to leave yet. Aggie had something to show her, so I thought it would be a good time to go looking for you."

"Looking for me?" He'd avoided her the entire time he'd been in the house, and now he had come looking for her?

"I wanted to talk to you," he said.

"They'll be wondering where you've gone off to." She moved, intending to step around him.

He reached out and barred her way with his arm. "I think they'll guess."

Her breath caught. Even in the near dark, she could see something in his eyes. Something familiar. "What did you want to talk to me about?"

He dropped his arm and kept his voice low. "I just wanted you to know that this was all Hettie's doing."

She held her head high and did her best to keep her voice from wobbling with emotion. "I'd already figured that out."

"Yeah, I guess you would. It's just that... Well, I

didn't want you to get the wrong idea and get your hopes up that…"

She waited for him to finish, and when he didn't, she did it for him. "That I would think you wanted us to get back together? To pick up where we left off? I can assure you I know better. You made that perfectly clear earlier." Once again, she attempted to get past him, and again he stopped her.

"Don't do this, Trish."

"*Don't do this?* You have the nerve to say that to me after—" She stopped herself. She wasn't going to put herself through this again. He had already told her how he felt. He blamed her. For what, she didn't know. Had it been because she'd wanted to take advantage of a rare opportunity to see a little of the country and meet the people in it? She'd sacrificed part of her teaching year, in addition to delaying her wedding plans. Her decision might not have pleased him, but she was glad she'd made it. And she was seeing a side to Morgan she hadn't known existed. Maybe it was better this way, but it certainly wasn't the best timing.

He stuffed his hands into the pockets of his blue jeans, a sure sign that he was having problems with saying what he wanted to say. "I just want you to know that I still—" he began without looking at her. Slowly, he raised his gaze to hers. "I still care about you, Trish, and that's why this is so hard. I don't want you to get the wrong idea, because I don't want you to be hurt."

She opened her mouth to tell him she'd already been hurt, possibly far more than he could guess, but he'd turned and walked away.

She watched as he disappeared into the kitchen. She heard her aunt and Hettie chiding him for having been missing, and she stayed out of sight until she knew he had driven away, Hettie with him.

He'd made it clear it was over between them. But it wasn't. She needed to tell him she was very likely pregnant, but he was making it impossible for her to discuss it. Maybe for now, and until she was sure, it was best to say nothing.

Chapter Two

"Don't let me forget the almonds for the marzipan," Kate said as she and Aggie got out of Trish's car.

"Didn't you put it on the shopping list?" Aggie asked.

"Does she ever?" Trish said, laughing. Her sister was the worst with lists. It was a wonder she was able to pull together a wedding as quickly as she had in less than six months.

Aggie closed the car door and pulled a crumpled paper from her back pocket. "Give me a pen, Trish. I'll add it."

With a sigh, Trish dug in her purse, found a pen and handed it to her aunt. "Did you add a stop at the post office for Kate's package?"

Aggie scanned the scrap of paper. "Yep, it's here." Scribbling what was probably the word *almonds,* she grunted. "This list is going to take us all day."

Kate stepped up onto the sidewalk near the Chick-a-Lick Café, and the others followed. "That's why I suggested we eat in town. I know how you get after a meal."

She looked pointedly at Aunt Aggie, who shrugged her shoulders. "When you're my age, you won't be so full of energy, my girl."

"My energy is about depleted," Kate said with a loud sigh. "This wedding can't come soon enough. I'm longing to get on that cruise ship and do nothing but sleep."

"And I'm sure that's exactly what you'll be doing," Aggie said, winking at Trish.

Trish's reply was a laugh as she opened the door to the café. But her laughter died when she noticed Morgan sitting at one of the tables. She'd known it would happen. It would be foolish to think it wouldn't. In Desperation, you could always count on seeing the last person you wanted to see.

"Let's sit over there," Kate said, pointing to the table next to Morgan's.

Before Trish could protest, Kate had hurried over and pulled out a chair. "Good afternoon, Sheriff," she said.

"Miss Clayborne," he replied with a brief smile and a nod. "All the Miss Claybornes, that is. What brings you into town today?"

"Wedding errands," Aggie replied with a grunt as she sat on the nearest chair. "Enough to keep us here until sundown."

Trish didn't fail to notice that her aunt and sister had given her only two choices. She could sit with her back to Morgan, giving him the satisfaction of not having to look at her, or she could sit on the other side of the table where they'd be forced to endure each other.

"Sit down, Trish," Aggie said, pulling out and indicating the chair that would mean there'd be no way to avoid him.

Let him suffer, Trish thought as she took her seat and grabbed one of the plastic-coated menus. Instead of hiding behind it, she opened it and laid it flat in front of her. Just let him try to ignore her. He'd soon find folks in Desperation would notice and have plenty to gossip about. But she instantly remembered she might soon be giving them lots to talk about.

Flashing her best smile—a smile she knew would show off her dimples—she looked directly at Morgan. "Have you caught any speeders today, Sheriff?"

He looked up, surprise in his eyes, and shook his head. "Slow day, slow drivers."

"Maybe it'll pick up," she said with a nonchalant shrug of one shoulder. "We wouldn't want you to get bored."

The look he gave her stalled her heart. "Never bored, not in Desperation," he replied. "Especially not in present company."

Trish was grateful that Darla chose that moment to take their orders. Trish turned her attention to her menu, doing her best not to dissect Morgan's words. He was usually a plainspoken man of few words, but at that moment, she wasn't sure what to think.

"Trish?"

Jarred from her thoughts, Trish looked at Kate. "What?"

Kate gave a covert glance at Darla.

"Oh!" Trish could feel the heat of a blush on her face. "I'm sorry. I'll take the BLT and tea."

"That's sweet tea," Darla said, making a note on her pad.

"No, not sweet tea. Unsweetened, please. With a slice of lemon, if you have it."

Darla looked up from her pad and stared for several seconds. "If you say so." Walking away, she shook her head, clucked her tongue and said, "The strange things people pick up when they're away."

"I wonder what she would have thought if I'd ordered green tea," Trish said.

Aggie laughed out loud, turning heads in the process. "She'd have flat out hit the deck." Shaking her head, she made a face. "I don't know that I could abide unsweetened tea."

"I've been trying to cut out sugars," Trish explained.

Kate leaned forward. "I've heard green tea is good for you. Very healthy and can help with cholesterol and all that." She turned to Aggie. "Maybe you should try it."

"You'd like it with mint," Trish added. "Kate, do you have any mint extract?"

Aggie *harrumphed.* "I'll stick with my sweet tea. I've been drinking it all my life. In fact, I think my mama put it in my bottle."

"Now, Miss Aggie, it doesn't hurt to try something new."

Trish looked up to see Morgan standing over them. "She really should," she agreed, turning back to her aunt. "If you don't like it, Aunt Aggie, I'll drink it."

"Put it on the list, Aunt Aggie," Kate said. "And don't forget the mint extract."

"This list just gets longer and longer," Aggie muttered, but added the items to the paper.

"I see you all have this under control," Morgan said. "Enjoy your lunch, ladies." He touched the wide brim of his hat and turned to walk away.

"Oh, Morgan!" Kate called after him. "Don't forget the rehearsal on Friday night at six."

He stopped at the door and turned around. "Dinner afterward?"

"Of course."

"You cooking?"

"That's the rumor."

"I'll be there. You can count on it."

Kate laughed as he turned and opened the door. "I figured as much." When he was gone, she turned to Trish. "I really do wish you two would work things out. You couldn't find a better man." Her grin appeared, wiping out her concern. "Except for mine, that is."

Trish smiled for a brief moment. "I never said I could. But Morgan isn't interested. Didn't you notice?"

"I still say, let Dusty talk—"

"Absolutely not!" Trish realized she'd raised her voice when several people turned to look at them. "It wouldn't help, Kate," she said, her voice lowered. "He made his decision in October, and I don't intend to try to change his mind." After the things he'd said the night she'd returned home, she couldn't think of a reason why she should make the effort.

Through the café's large front window, Trish could see Morgan talking to one of the local ranchers. Her appetite vanished, along with the man who had recently made her want to chew nails. But the situation wasn't over yet and would probably get worse before it got better—if it ever *did* get better.

She tried her best to participate in the conversation, but her mind was on other things. When they were finished and leaving the café, she knew this would be her only chance to escape.

"You two go ahead and start on the list," she told them as they stood outside in front of the café, discussing what to do first. "I have a quick errand to run, and I'll be back in a little while."

"Where?" Kate asked.

"Just over to Kingfisher. I saw something there I wanted to get for the wedding. It won't take long, I promise, and then I'll be back to help finish the errands."

"You can't get it in Desperation?" Aggie asked.

Trish shook her head. She didn't want to say any more than she had to.

Kate shrugged and glanced at Aggie. "I guess we can handle it. Don't take too long though, Trish. I'd hate to have to call Dusty for a ride home. He's up to his ears helping Tanner get everything in order with the stock company before we leave."

"No longer than it has to take, I promise," Trish said, moving to her car. When the two had walked away, she climbed in, started the engine and backed out of the parking space. If she could have done this errand in Desperation, she would have, but she didn't need anyone seeing her purchase the item she needed.

MORGAN WASN'T LOOKING FORWARD to the wedding rehearsal. He'd pretty much known Trish would be back for her sister's wedding, but he'd hoped something— anything—might keep her from coming back too soon. And the other night had been too soon for him. If only canceling their wedding had canceled his feelings.

Opening the door to the Commune the next evening, he stepped inside the entry hall. His job as the town sheriff wasn't difficult, but before he'd come home, he'd had to lock up John Rutgers for making a scene at Lou's Place, the local tavern. John was a good man, but when he started drinking, he got mean. Mean enough last June to hold a pistol to—

From farther down the hallway, he heard a door open. With his foot on the first step of the stairs leading up to his apartment, he stopped.

"I'll be back to help with dinner, Freda," his uncle was saying to the Commune's cook.

The door closed and Morgan managed two more steps before Ernie called to him. "There you are. Come on into the kitchen with me while I check on dinner."

Morgan didn't feel up to a conversation with his uncle. "I'd like to shower and change," he said, hoping that would be the end of it.

Resting his hand on the newel post, Ernie looked up at him. "I heard you ran into the Claybornes at the café."

"I did. Don't think I hurt them, though."

Ernie chuckled. "'Course you didn't." He looked around and then met Morgan's gaze, his expression solemn. "I also heard you had to take John in."

"Word travels fast," Morgan answered with a wry smile. "I could really use that shower, and then I'll have to take something over for John to eat, so if you don't—"

"Ernie, who are you talking to?"

Morgan had to bite the inside of his cheek to keep from groaning. Hettie had ears like a bat.

Ernie pressed a finger to his lips. "Just talking to myself, Hettie." Crooking the same finger at Morgan, he motioned for him to follow.

Morgan followed him down the hall to the Commune's office and his uncle's private apartment. "You can shower here," Ernie told him. "Freda left a load of laundry in the kitchen, and I saw some of your things in it. You shower, I'll get your clothes."

"Thanks," Morgan said as he tossed his hat to a nearby chair and strode to the bathroom, stripping off his clothes as he went. When his shower was finished, he found the clothes Ernie had brought, dressed in worn jeans and a T-shirt, pinned on his badge and grabbed his hat and jacket.

He was reaching for the doorknob when the door opened and his uncle walked in, a covered tray in his hands and a large thermos under one arm. "Freda got John's supper together while you were in the shower," Ernie explained. When Morgan started to take the tray from him, Ernie shook his head. "Have a seat," he said, indicating the sofa with a nod. "I've been meaning to talk to you. It won't take long."

With a shrug, Morgan sat on the sofa while Ernie set the tray and thermos aside.

"Is everything okay with John?" Ernie asked as he settled in his easy chair.

Morgan dipped his chin in a nod. "He's behaving. Not that he hasn't been drinking, though."

"It's only been that one time, right?"

Meeting his gaze, Morgan nodded again. "Like I said, he's behaving."

Ernie was silent for a moment, then he shifted in his seat. "Maybe it's time to tell Trish what happened."

"No."

"You can't keep the truth from her," Ernie said, his voice low. "You're not being fair to her."

Morgan stared at him. "Fair? Was it fair when some hoodlums gunned Ben down in his own front yard? In front of his wife?"

Ernie shook his head and sighed. "No, it wasn't. But that doesn't mean you should live a lie and force Trish to live one, too."

"I'd rather she believes I'm heartless."

"You don't mean that."

"I do mean it," Morgan insisted.

"It's time to put the past to rest and move forward."

"I did that when I came to Desperation. I believed bad things didn't happen here," Morgan admitted, although it wasn't easy. "When I asked Trish to marry me, I'd thought those old memories were fading and I'd found some peace. But when John pulled that gun on me, all I could think of was that night in Miami. I swore then that I'd never put a woman through what Connie went through. I meant it."

"The thing with John was a one-time thing," Ernie said. "A fluke."

"And who's to say there won't be another situation? Maybe John, maybe someone else. There's no guarantee."

"Nobody has a guarantee."

Morgan understood what his uncle was saying, but for him, it didn't matter. He'd rather see Trish with someone else than for her to become his widow. He loved her too much to risk letting that happen.

Getting to his feet, he avoided looking at Ernie. "I need to get that food to John."

Ernie stood, too, and reached out to give Morgan's shoulder a comforting squeeze. "Think about it. That's all I'm asking."

Nodding, but knowing there was nothing to think about, Morgan took the supper Freda had prepared for the prisoner and left the apartment.

He had his hand on the old brass door handle of the entrance to the Commune and was about to open the door when he heard Hettie.

"Are you leaving? I didn't know you were here."

"Yeah, I need to get this food to the jail."

"But the committee is here," Hettie said from behind him.

He turned to her, completely at a loss. "What committee?"

Hettie sighed. "I can't believe you've forgotten. I asked you three weeks ago to be on the committee planning the New Year's Eve party. We'll need help with some of the decorations."

"Well, I forgot. And I'm sorry but—"

Trish appeared in the hallway behind Hettie, not looking particularly pleased. She glanced at Hettie, whose back was to her, and her frown deepened. Morgan sensed she wasn't happy with their friend, either.

He'd had enough of Hettie's matchmaking efforts. "You'll have to do it without me. I have dinner to take to—"

"Now, Morgan…"

He knew he was about to lose his temper, but he didn't seem to be able to stop himself. "No, Hettie—"

"Hettie, please," Trish interrupted. "We don't need him. I'm sure there's someone else who's willing and free to help."

"But—" Hettie began, and then stopped.

Defeat was written all over her face, and Morgan felt awful for treating her badly. "I won't be gone long," he said.

Trish took a step forward. "You don't have to worry that I'll be here when you get back. I need to get home," she explained and glanced at Hettie. "The meeting is nearly over, and I'm sure Aunt Aggie and Kate are expecting me home soon."

"Drive carefully," he told her, meaning it. Now that she was driving, he worried about her, especially on the dirt country roads at night.

Quickly slipping out the door, he sucked in a deep breath of cold night air on the way to his cruiser and felt better. As he drove the few blocks to the town jail, he thought about Hettie's persistence, but he wouldn't let it get to him. The clock couldn't be turned back to a happier time.

He parked the cruiser and walked into the City Building where all the city offices were located, including his, and the jail. He made quick work of checking on the prisoner and his deputy. Not wanting to stay long and listen to John's complaining, he returned to his car.

The drive back to the Commune gave him just enough time to revisit Hettie's arguments, confirming his belief that there was nothing left to talk about. He'd made his decision six weeks ago, the night before Trish had left on her tour—the night he'd broken their engagement and canceled their wedding. He didn't owe anyone an explanation—especially Hettie.

"EVERYONE MAKE CERTAIN you stay clear of the candles," Theda Baker, the minister's wife, said, lining up the bridesmaids in the brown winter grass. Headlights from several vehicles lit the area of the park around the large gazebo where the wedding would take place the next evening. "I know the candles aren't here this evening, but they'll be lining the main aisle tomorrow night, and we don't want someone bumping into them and having the whole town going up in smoke. And where have Greta and Travis gone to?"

"Right here," Trish answered, standing with Kate's six-year-old flower girl and ring bearer. "Come on, kids," she told them, taking them by the hand. "Mrs. Baker is going to give us our instructions for tomorrow night."

Tomorrow night. The thought made Trish's head spin as she placed Greta and Travis in front of Terry Tartelli, Kate's stand-in, according to tradition. So much had happened since Kate had announced she and Dusty were engaged and there would be a Christmas wedding. They'd had so little time to plan everything, yet here they were, with the wedding only one day away. Her own wedding would have been over and done with, and she'd be a happily married woman, if she hadn't gone on tour and Morgan hadn't canceled the wedding. But she was determined not to let any of that spoil the joy of her sister's wedding.

In front of the gazebo, Dusty stood with his best man and business partner, Tanner O'Brien, while the ushers, Morgan and Jimmy Tartelli, waited off to the side. Trish could tell Morgan was doing everything he could to keep from looking at her. After Morgan had canceled the wedding, Kate had asked if having him as an usher would be a problem. Trish had told her it wouldn't. Now she wished she'd told her to find someone else.

"Fran, if you'll start the processional…" Mrs. Baker said, signaling the musician, who sat at a small portable organ. Turning to the wedding party as the first strains of music rang out, she smiled. "All right, girls, are we ready?"

Trish moved into position and looked around.

Seventeen-year-old Shawn O'Brien, Tanner's nephew, was missing. "Shawn isn't here yet," she pointed out.

"He's at basketball practice," Jules, Tanner's wife, said from her spot ahead of Trish. "He'll be here as soon as he can, but you know how the coach is about his players."

Mrs. Baker, obviously not convinced, looked to her husband, who stood inside the gazebo. "It's all right, Theda, we'll just use a stand-in until he gets here," the reverend told her as the strains of the processional died out. "Sheriff Rule, would you mind standing in for the young man?"

Trish didn't miss how Morgan glanced toward the street. He was clearly not fond of the idea, but he stood and joined Dusty and Tanner at the steps of the gazebo.

"All right," Mrs. Baker called out. "Fran, if you would start again?"

For the second time, the music began, and Mrs. Baker cued Jules to start her walk down the aisle. A few musical bars later, Trish followed.

She and Kate had spent hours choosing music, intent on not duplicating anything for the two weddings being planned to take place only two months apart. It suddenly struck her that her choices would never be played—at least at her own wedding—and she felt a sadness that nearly overwhelmed her.

Don't think about it. Just don't.

She reached her place at the gazebo and turned to see her sister watching the rehearsal, a nervous smile playing on her lips. She caught Trish's eye and winked. Kate had always been the tomboy of the two of them and had at first tried to talk Dusty into eloping. Trish blessed him for insisting they do it the old-fashioned way. Tonight Kate looked like the epitome of the blushing but nervous bride—a bride in blue jeans, boots and a Sherpa jacket, her long auburn braid tossed over one shoulder. Trish instantly forgot her own troubles and returned her sister's mischievous wink.

Reverend Baker took over the rehearsal and explained each step of the ceremony. Five minutes later, a shout was heard.

"Sorry I'm late. Blame Coach," Shawn called out, rushing to join the rest of the wedding party. "Where do you want me?"

"Here," Morgan said, quickly stepping back and indicating the spot where he'd stood. He moved away to where the last row of the chairs would be, even before Shawn rushed to take his place.

"We're glad you could make it, Shawn," Reverend Baker told him. "How's the team doing this year?"

"Good," Shawn answered, looking a bit embarrassed that the spotlight was still on him.

"Glad to hear it. I was just running through the steps of the ceremony," Reverend Baker explained. "Now that you're here, we'll go through them again quickly for everyone. I'm sure you'll catch on."

Trish focused on the Reverend's instructions. The last thing she wanted to do was mess up during her sister's wedding. And it helped her forget, if only for a little while, that Morgan was there, watching.

"Any questions?" Reverend Baker asked. "No? Then we're done. Try to get some rest tonight, although I know for some of you it won't be easy."

"Please come to the rehearsal dinner, Reverend," Kate urged.

Reverend Baker glanced around the area. "You have many friends to help make it a memorable night, Kate. I'm sure I won't be missed. But thank you again for the invitation."

Tanner was talking to Morgan, but stopped. "It's Kate's cooking, Reverend. Are you sure you want to miss it?"

Reverend Baker tipped his head back and laughed, the sound filling the dark evening. "The temptation is strong, but I'll still beg off."

Trish watched as Kate stepped up and gave the older man a kiss on his cheek. "Thank you for everything."

"It's my pleasure, Kate," he said.

Turning around, Kate looked over the group waiting for instructions. "Fifteen minutes, everybody. Don't let the food get cold." Looping her arm through Trish's, she led her back up the makeshift aisle to the park's entrance. "It went well, I'd say. Now let's hope the wedding goes off without a snag."

"It will," Trish replied, "and everyone in Desperation will be talking about it for months."

Kate laughed. "That's what I'm afraid of."

They were interrupted by Dusty, who swept Kate into his arms and gave her a noisy kiss. Friends chuckled in the background, and Trish eased away.

Dusty touched her arm, stopping her. "Where are you going?"

Needing to escape, if only for a few minutes, Trish stepped back. "I think I'll go on to the café and see if they need any help setting up."

Dusty shook his head, then jammed his cowboy hat lower onto his head. Still keeping an arm around his bride-to-be, he took Trish's arm. "Nope. That's not the job of the maid of honor. They have plenty of help over at the café. Aggie made sure of that. And you're going to walk over with us."

"But—"

"No buts," Kate said, her stern voice sounding much like Aunt Aggie's. "I know this isn't easy for you, what with Morgan here and everything, but I want you to enjoy yourself tonight."

"I'm fine," Trish assured her, not wanting to worry her sister at the most important time of her life.

Kate studied her closely, but spoke to Dusty. "Would you mind giving us a few minutes?"

Dusty appeared to be put out, but his quick smile made a lie of it. "In a little over twenty-four hours, you'll be all mine, so, no, I don't mind. Just don't be long."

"Is something wrong?" Trish asked, after he'd given Kate a quick kiss and strolled away to join the other men.

"I don't know. You tell me."

Trish felt a cold rush of dread. "About what?"

Kate looked around and moved closer. "I found something in the bathroom. Do you want to tell me something?"

Surprised her secret had been discovered and embarrassed that it had, Trish couldn't make eye contact with her sister. There was only one thing Kate might have found and questioned. "The pregnancy test," she said, knowing it could be nothing else.

Kate nodded and waited.

"Well, now you know."

Shaking her head, Kate smiled. "I only know you have a test. Is that what you went to Kingfisher to get?"

Nodding, Trish kept her eyes on the toes of her shoes.

"Smart move. There's no reason to alert everyone in Desperation. Have you taken the test?"

Trish still couldn't look her in the eye. "This morning."

Taking Trish's hand in hers, Kate forced her to look up.

"By your response, I'm assuming it was positive?"

Trish nodded again.

"There's nothing to be ashamed of, you know."

"I know," Trish replied, but she knew that not everyone saw it that way.

Kate chuckled softly. "Good, because if you did feel ashamed, we'd both have to be, and I'm certainly not."

Trish stared at her. "*You're* pregnant?"

"Just a little, if that's possible," she said, laughing as Trish hugged her, "and the timing couldn't be worse. I hope I can bypass the morning sickness, but I have a feeling being on a cruise ship will only make it worse." Her sigh was a whisper as people moved past them. "You haven't told Morgan, have you?"

Shaking her head, Trish tried her best to hold back the tears that threatened. Along with everything else, her emotions were bouncing back and forth like a ping-pong ball. "I don't know when to tell him. Not with everything that's going on."

"But you will. Soon. Right?"

Unable to speak, Trish nodded.

"If you need me to be there—"

"No. I can do it myself. And I don't want it interfering with your wedding."

Kate turned and looked around at the nearly empty park. "I guess we'd better get to the café. Dusty will be wondering what's keeping us." Looping her arm through Trish's again, she started walking, taking Trish with her. "What do you think about telling Aunt Aggie together?"

"I think it's a good idea," Trish answered. But it was only right that she tell Morgan first.

One night. That's all it had taken, and their lives had been changed forever. Afterward, she and Morgan had argued about her tour, but she hadn't backed down. She hadn't known then what she would be facing in only a few weeks. And that's when he had told her the wedding was off—with no explanation. Baby or no baby, she deserved an explanation, and she intended to get one.

Chapter Three

From his position next to the antique horse-drawn carriage that Kate and her bridesmaids had ridden in to her wedding, Morgan could hear and see every bit of the ceremony—including a clear view of Trish. He wished he couldn't.

"Sheriff?"

Morgan looked back to see his deputy. "Everything okay?"

Stu nodded. "Nice and quiet." He turned toward where the wedding vows were being exchanged. "Dusty and Kate got lucky."

"How's that?" Morgan asked, not that he disagreed. Dusty McPherson and Kate were perfectly matched. Everyone in Desperation was happy to see them getting married. Because most of the people in town had witnessed Dusty's marriage proposal, after he'd lassoed her at the Fourth of July celebration, the whole town had been invited to the event, and it looked as though Desperation's entire population had turned out for it.

"Couldn't ask for nicer weather a week from Christmas," Stu answered.

"Yeah." Morgan looked up at the starry sky and the nearly full moon shining down on the ceremony and adding a shimmer to the second light snow that month.

When neither of them said anything for several minutes, Stu moved away. "Guess I'd better go make sure it stays nice and quiet around here. You going to the reception?"

Wishing he could avoid another Clayborne family event, Morgan knew he had no choice, and he nodded. "I'm supposed to be there. Won't be for long, though."

Stu nodded in understanding and walked away, leaving Morgan wondering how the reception would turn out. He planned to skip the dinner and dance afterward, if at all possible. In fact, he'd done pretty well avoiding as much as he could throughout the wedding hubbub. The thought of weddings made him want to punch something. And he had never been a violent man.

In spite of what some people might think, he loved Trish and suspected he always would. But he couldn't subject her to the real possibility that something could happen to him. She didn't deserve that.

Lost in thoughts of what might have been, he was startled when the music began again, signaling the end of the ceremony. He waited beside the horse until the bride and groom approached. After helping Kate into the carriage, he turned to find himself face-to-face with Trish. Unable to think of anything to say, he offered her his hand for assistance. She barely glanced at him, but thanked him quietly when she had settled on the seat in back. Jules O'Brien, Kate's bridesmaid, followed, and he did the same for her.

"Morgan?"

Ready to head for his car now that the ceremony was

over, he turned back to see Kate lean in front of her new husband.

"We'll see you at the reception, right?" she asked.

"Yes, ma'am," he answered, touching his finger to the brim of his hat in salute and adding a smile. He had always liked Kate. She was all spit and fire. And since Dusty, who'd spent most of his life on the rodeo circuit, had returned to Desperation several months before, the two men had become friends. Along with Tanner O'Brien, they'd shared a few beers at Lou's Place, talked guy-talk and had some good times. It hadn't seemed to make any difference to them that he had called off the wedding and wouldn't be marrying Trish. He'd hoped it wouldn't. He valued their friendships. He just didn't let himself get too personal or too close to people. Miami had taught him well.

After driving the two blocks to the old Opera House, where the wedding reception was being held, Morgan checked his watch before getting out of his patrol car. There was still an hour to go before he would take over the rest of the night shift for Stu. He'd promised his deputy the night off to attend the dinner and dance later that night. Morgan didn't mind missing either. He'd never been one to socialize, and now he had even less desire to do so.

In the final stages of renovation, the inside of the Opera House was decked out in flowers and greenery for both the upcoming holiday and the wedding. Guests crowded the long hallway, and he followed them into the theater, still without seats, where the bride and groom and their wedding party were laughing and chatting with all. Morgan didn't see the need to join them and instead headed for a table containing the punch bowl. He had just filled the small glass cup when he felt someone touch his arm.

"Dusty said to tell you there's a keg of beer set up in my accounting office," Kate told him when he turned to look at her.

"Sounds good," he said, "but I'll be on duty again in less than an hour."

The shadow of a frown crossed her face. "Are you trying to avoid us? You know that isn't necessary."

He hated that she had pegged him on it, but he really did have a legitimate excuse. "I promised Stu he could have the time off to go to the dinner and dance. It only seemed fair."

"Of course it is," she said with a smile. "You've always been a fair man. About most things."

Nobody had to explain to him what she was getting at. "Look, Kate—"

"There you are," Dusty called out. "They're getting ready to start taking pictures. We'd better get a move on."

"I'll be right there," she told him. Then she turned back to Morgan. "We'll need you for the formal pictures. Wedding party and all that."

Before he could answer, someone claimed her attention. He moved on, wishing one more time that he had excused himself from being a part of the wedding.

Spying his uncle, he made his way through the crowd of guests and finally stood beside him. "I guess it's all over except the shouting," he said.

Ernie looked at him. "Not even close. I'm looking forward to the dinner. I heard Kate had a hand in it."

"Probably more than just a hand," Morgan answered. "From what I heard, she was out at the Blue Barn making sure everything was being fixed to her specifications and didn't leave until about an hour before the wedding."

Smiling, Ernie nodded. "That sounds like Kate. I heard Trish was a big help. Aggie said she's gotten the hang of cooking."

Determined not to be pulled into a conversation about Trish, Morgan didn't answer. When he had first started seriously seeing her, it was a running joke that she couldn't even boil water, while her sister had a natural talent in the kitchen. Since then, Kate had been busy teaching Trish, who had taken to it pretty well.

When Morgan saw Hettie heading their way, his first reaction was to leave, but he reminded himself that as long as he didn't argue with her, she would think he agreed, even if he didn't.

"Well, Morgan, what do you think?" Hettie asked when she reached them. "Is the whole town here tonight or what?"

Seeing that it was an innocent question, he felt safe in answering. "Sure seems so."

"It was a beautiful wedding, wasn't it?"

He shrugged, and then realized he should be agreeing. But what did he know about weddings?

"Oh, you men," Hettie said, laughing. "You wouldn't know a good wedding from a bad one, even if you were the one getting married."

To his relief, Kate reappeared. "I know you have to leave," she told him, "but stop by the party later, if you can. We still consider you a good friend and practically part of the family."

The Claybornes were good people, some of the best around, and Kate had just managed to make him feel like a heel, which was exactly how he had been acting. "Thanks, Kate," he said sincerely. "That means a lot." And he silently vowed to be nicer to Trish.

"AND WE'LL WANT one of Aggie and Hettie," Trish told the photographer. She looked around the crowded theater, wondering what was keeping Kate. And Morgan.

"Do you want to start with them, then?" the photographer asked. "Seeing that the bride isn't here yet, I mean."

Dusty crossed the stage to where Trish was standing. "Where *is* Kate, anyway?" His eyebrows drew together as he glanced toward the crowd of friends in the theater. "Never mind," he said, smiling. "There she is."

Trish turned to watch her younger sister hurrying to the stairs at the side of the stage. Kate wasn't the type to care about being a traditional beautiful bride, but she had outdone herself on her special day, and Trish smiled at the picture she made.

"Sorry I'm late," Kate said breathlessly, the front hem of her long dress hiked to her knees as she climbed the steps to the stage. Smiling at the man with the camera, she said, "Whenever you're ready. We're only waiting on one, and he wasn't far behind me."

Trish gathered all the others and helped make sure everyone who was to be in each photo was ready and waiting. The deep red velvet curtains were pulled across the main stage, providing a backdrop, with tall candelabras and flowers strategically placed.

Trish was so busy, she didn't notice Morgan walk up until he spoke. "Where do you want me?" he asked.

She spun around to find him standing on the floor below at the front edge of the stage. Surprised, she lost her train of thought. "I don't— I'll have to find out how soon they want the entire wedding party together."

"Okay. I'll wait over there." He moved to take a seat on a chair at the side of the room, near the stage, crossed one foot over the other knee, and spread his arms out over the back of the chairs beside him. He seemed completely at ease.

For a moment, Trish stared at him. Without the frown he'd recently been wearing, she wasn't sure what she should think.

"We'll get the bridesmaids and groomsmen next, then add the flower girl and ring bearer, and after that, the entire wedding party," the photographer said.

After taking several pictures, the photographer turned to the house, where some of the guests stood watching. "Are the ushers here?" he asked.

"Here," Jimmy said, as he and Morgan walked up the steps and onto the stage to join the others. The photographer arranged the positions of the wedding party and took several pictures. When he was done, they were all dismissed.

Before everyone wandered away, Dusty reminded them that the dinner and dance at the Blue Barn would start in an hour and encouraged everyone to attend.

"There'll be a crowd," Jimmy said. "Count on it."

Tanner laughed. "They all want to see the inside of the place."

Dusty laughed with him. "My grandmother always called it a den of iniquity. I guess everyone wants to make sure it is." He turned to Morgan. "You're going to be there, aren't you?"

"I'll try to stop by for a few minutes," Morgan answered, "but I won't be able to stay long. No telling what some crazy kid might decide to try while everyone's busy."

"The sheriff's work is never done, eh, Morgan?" Tanner asked.

Morgan shrugged. "I can't complain."

Standing nearby, Trish watched her former betrothed as he told everyone goodbye and left. She knew she had to tell him soon about the baby. Before long, she would be showing, and everyone would know. That wasn't the way she wanted him to find out. But she needed to do it at the right time and place, and a building full of people attending her sister's wedding wasn't it.

Ready to leave, she moved through the remaining guests to the door leading out of the theater. In the hallway, she found her aunt and Hettie. "We should go on to the Blue Barn," she told them. "Kate might need some help with the dinner."

Aggie and Hettie gathered their things and followed Trish out of the building. "I didn't hear a single person say they weren't going. I hope Kate and Dusty anticipate a big crowd," Hettie commented.

Aggie, walking on the other side of Trish, laughed. "Oh, I'm sure they do."

"What I want to know," Hettie said, "is why they chose the Blue Barn. It's nothing more than a honky-tonk, although a famous one around these parts, I admit."

"Wouldn't *notorious* be a better word?" Trish asked, grinning. Nothing could raise her spirits more than having Aggie and Hettie around.

"Believe it or not, Hettie," Aggie said, as they reached the car, "the Blue Barn played an integral part in getting Kate and Dusty together." She winked at Trish, who opened the passenger door for her and circled around to her own. "And I can proudly say I was a part of that."

Hettie waited while Aggie climbed into the small backseat. "I seem to remember you telling me something about sending him there to find her."

Aggie laughed as Hettie slid into the front seat next to Trish. "Ask Kate about it sometime. Or better yet, ask Dusty."

Trish scooted in behind the steering wheel and started the car, chuckling at the memory of how she and Aggie had convinced Kate to wear a dress on her first visit to the Blue Barn and how Dusty had reacted to seeing her there.

"You look tired," Hettie told her.

Trish smiled, the effort itself tiring. "It's been a long day, and it isn't over yet."

Aggie agreed. "It's going to be an even longer night, but I wouldn't miss it for the world. It's not every day that one of my nieces gets married."

Knowing her aunt hadn't meant to remind her of her canceled wedding, Trish smiled and nodded. "I don't want to miss it, either."

Hettie turned her head to look at Trish. "There's something I've been meaning to talk to you about."

"What's that?" Trish asked, turning onto the county road.

"About Christmas Eve. I want both you and Aggie to come spend it with me at the Commune."

So wrapped up in getting home from her tour, and then in Kate's wedding, not to mention wondering when and how she'd tell Morgan about the baby, Trish hadn't given much thought to Christmas plans. But she wasn't sure she wanted to spend the evening at the Commune.

Morgan was bound to be there, and with the way things were going between them, spending Christmas Eve in his company wasn't her idea of a pleasant evening. "I don't know, Hettie…."

"We'll go to the candle-lighting service at the church, of course," Hettie went on, before Trish could say more. "Kate was so nice to make up some cookie dough and freeze it. Freda is going to bake them, along with some wonderful Swedish dishes for the smorgasbord. We do so want you and Aggie both to join us."

"It's going to be strange not to have Kate with us this year," Aggie said with a sigh from the backseat.

"Ernie and Freda have had their heads together, planning everything," Hettie continued. "Please say you'll come, Trish. It would mean so much to me."

Trish couldn't refuse Hettie's request. Next to Aunt Aggie, Hettie had been like a second mother. The women were such opposites, much like she and Kate were, that it was sometimes comical to watch them together. And they both expected their words to be law and their wishes to be granted.

"Of course I'll be there," she said. "Aunt Aggie is right, it won't be Christmas with just the two of us. Sharing it with everyone at the Commune will be fun and make up for Kate being gone on her honeymoon." Somehow she'd get through it *and* enjoy herself.

They arrived at the Blue Barn and helped Kate with little chores before people began arriving. Once the first of the guests arrived and the crowd grew, Trish was too busy to do anything except try to enjoy it all. As the evening wore on, she became more tired, but she was determined to see it through to the end. She'd heard Morgan had been there for a few minutes, but she hadn't seen him. It was just as well. What she had to tell him had to be done in private.

When the time finally came for the bride and groom to be on their way, Kate pulled Trish aside. "I'll call you on New Year's Eve," Kate told her. "We'll be in port then. Maybe on Christmas, too, but I can't promise that."

Trish felt tears coming on and could only nod. She was already beginning to miss her sister.

"You haven't told Morgan yet, have you?" Kate asked.

Swallowing the lump of emotion in her throat, Trish answered. "Not yet, and I don't know if I'll see him before Christmas Eve. Aunt Aggie and I are supposed to spend it with Hettie at the Commune, and I expect Morgan will be there for at least part of the evening."

"Maybe Christmas Eve, then?" Kate asked gently. "What a present that could be!"

A vision of what Morgan's reaction might be popped into Trish's mind. "Or not," she said, feeling far from positive about it. "But it would be the best time."

"And the worst time for me to be gone," Kate said, her eyes filled with concern.

Trish tried for a smile. "I'm a big girl. I can handle it. And I'm the one who got myself into this."

"With a little help from Morgan," Kate reminded her. "You can't put it off, Trish. Not with Morgan, anyway. And with Aunt Aggie and Hettie leaving for their cruise after the first of the year…"

Sighing, Trish shook her head. "Let's wait to tell them when they get back. I don't want anything to interfere with their trip, and I'm afraid they both might feel they need to cancel and stay home with me. But you're right. I've put off telling Morgan for as long as I can. Christmas Eve may be my best chance."

Kate wrapped her in her arms and hugged her. "*Make* it the best chance, Trish."

Knowing she couldn't put it off, Trish nodded. "I'll try."

"Promise?"

"Promise."

BY THE END OF THE NEXT WEEK, the weather had turned colder and the wind blew the limbs of the bare trees back and forth. Winter had definitely set in around Desperation.

As Trish stepped out of the church on Christmas Eve, she pulled her knit cap farther down around her ears. Apprehension had grown by the day, and she'd been nervous about what she knew she must do that evening. Now that they were headed for the Commune, she hoped her nervous stomach didn't embarrass her or ruin the evening for everyone.

"That was a beautiful service, as always," Hettie said, walking on one side of Trish.

"I've never been to a Christmas Eve candle-lighting service that wasn't," Aggie agreed from the other side. "I'm glad we decided to walk."

Trish, who had been half listening to the conversation, spoke. "Your knee isn't bothering you?"

"Nope," Aggie answered. "Doc Priller prescribed some new pills for me, and they seem to be doing the trick."

"I'm so glad to hear it," Trish told her sincerely.

They chatted on about the wedding the week before and gossip in Desperation. Just the mention of gossip reminded Trish that she would soon be the subject of it, which led to a churning stomach at the prospect of what the rest of the evening would bring. By the time they reached the stone steps of the Commune, she was ready to turn around and run away from it all, but she knew that was childish. She couldn't put it off. And she wanted some answers. She only hoped it didn't mar the evening for anyone other than the two of them.

Freda greeted them at the door, her round cheeks rosy and her smile as bright as the sun. "Good. Good. Now I have my ladies here to help." She stepped back to let them through the door. "Trish, you're all right?"

Startled, Trish looked up, her stomach tightening. "Yes, I am. Why?" It was if Freda had sensed her secret.

Freda cocked her head to one side and then shook it, smiling. 'Nothing. You look a little tired."

Relief swept through Trish. "After-wedding letdown, I guess," she said with a smile.

"Yes, it has been so very busy. But only a few more days and life will be quiet."

Trish knew this wouldn't be the case. More than likely, life would be topsy-turvy for quite some time.

They followed Freda to the kitchen, where pot after pot simmered on the double stove. "Smells wonderful, Freda," Hettie said, sniffing the air.

Freda's grin widened. "Good. Good." She picked up a platter piled high with appetizers and handed it to Trish. "The guests will start with this, while we put the rest on the sideboard and the table in the dining room. It will take the edge off their hunger until we are ready."

Trish checked out the contents of the plate. "Meatballs?"

"*Köttbullar*," Freda answered, nodding. "Go on. Try one."

Picking up one of the small, round meatballs stuck with a toothpick, Trish nibbled. "Oh, yes," she said and popped the rest of it into her mouth, closing her eyes and savoring it.

"Is it all Swedish fare this year?" Aggie asked.

"Oh, no," Freda answered. "Only the *köttbullar* and *lussekatter*. That is Saint Lucia buns. And the *Risgryngröt*."

"What's reesgr…" Hettie laughed. "Whatever you said."

"Rice porridge. It is special."

"How's that?"

"You will see," Freda answered with a mysterious smile. She gave Trish a nudge. "Go. Take the tray. They are all in the library waiting. Hettie and Aggie and I will get everything set up for the smorgasbord. It won't take us long."

Trish would have rather stayed in the kitchen, but no one was giving her the choice. In the hallway, she found Ernie talking to Elaine and Harold Anderson, who had been the first couple to move into the Commune when it opened.

"Why, Trish, what have you brought us?" Elaine asked when she saw Trish approaching.

When she reached them, Trish held out the tray. "Freda's Swedish meatballs. Dinner will be ready soon, but you can enjoy these until then."

Harold turned to Ernie. "I've always wondered where

you found Freda. She's a wonder in the kitchen. Keeps us all well fed."

"I met her on my travels," Ernie answered. "There wasn't a better cook in all of Sweden, and she was eager to see America. It was one of those win-win things for both of us." He turned to Trish. "Go on in. Everybody is gathered in the library."

Ernie opened the door to the library, and Trish stepped inside to find the room crowded with people. "*Köttbullar,* anyone?"

Knowing all the residents of the Commune and their families, she spoke to each person. She was fully aware that Morgan was among them, but tried to avoid looking at him. Her stomach was fluttering, and she had to make an effort to calm her racing heart. Anticipation, she reminded herself, was usually worse than the deed.

Ready to put that deed into motion, she approached Morgan, who stood near the blazing fireplace, a cup of eggnog in his hand. "I hope that's the nonalcoholic version," she teased with a smile she hoped didn't wobble.

"It's the only way to drink it when I know I'll be on duty later." He took a meatball from the tray and bit into it. "Mmm. These are fantastic," he exclaimed as he took another.

Nodding, she took a breath. "We need to talk."

He glanced around the room before looking at her directly. "Okay. Now?"

"Later, after dinner."

"I can do that. But just so you know, I have to make rounds."

"It won't take long." She couldn't even muster a smile and left him with a puzzled look on his face. She was halfway across the room on unsteady legs when Ernie walked in to announce that dinner was ready.

Although she participated in the evening's festivities, including the scrumptious smorgasbord Freda had prepared, Trish's evening passed by in a blur—until she found the almond in her pudding.

"According to tradition," Freda had announced when Trish discovered the surprise in her dish, "the person to find the almond is to marry in the coming year."

Trish barely commented. All she could think about was the task that awaited her when dinner was over.

The company was almost as good as being with her family, and she didn't miss Kate as much as she thought she might. She was wondering how Kate and Dusty were enjoying their honeymoon cruise when she saw Morgan speak to Ernie. He glanced at her, nodded, and then slipped out of the room. Excusing herself, she followed and found him waiting for her in the hallway.

"Is this a good time?" He glanced at his watch. "I have maybe fifteen minutes."

"Fifteen minutes is fine," she said, her throat closing on the words.

Crooking her finger for him to follow, she led him farther down the hall, away from the main rooms of the Commune. When they came to the small nook under the stairs, she took a deep breath to steady herself, unsure if her legs were going to hold her, and stepped into the shadows. Morgan followed. She felt light-headed and took another deep breath.

"I'm pregnant."

Time seemed to stand still. Morgan was looking at her, his eyes a little wider than usual, his face pale and his mouth open as if he'd been ready to say something. But there was nothing coming out.

He blinked once, then again. Closing his mouth, he gave a small shake of his head. "Pregnant?"

Trish prayed the dark edges of the room wouldn't take over everything in her vision, and then everything cleared. She nodded.

Chapter Four

Morgan stared at Trish, the woman he'd loved—and still loved, in spite of knowing he shouldn't. Her fair skin was paler than normal, and he guessed his probably was, too.

"When?" he finally managed to ask. The fact that she wasn't saying anything bothered him. "There's no way," he continued, shaking his head. "We didn't…"

And then he remembered.

"You're right," Trish said. "We didn't."

For one brief second, he almost believed nothing had happened, that they hadn't made love. But they had. He'd provoked an argument with her the night before she left on her tour, knowing that for her sake he had to break it off with her. But knowing it would all be over between them when she returned, he had gone beyond his own limits, and the argument had led to making love.

Now he understood why she had said they didn't. She'd meant they didn't take precautions.

He leaned against the wall for support as he closed his eyes and groaned, in spite of trying to stop it. Slowly opening them, he saw her watching him.

"Then you remember," she said.

He nodded and straightened. "Yes, I remember." He

waited for her to say more, but she remained silent. He knew he had treated her badly that night. Did she think he would run from his responsibility? Could he blame her if she did? He certainly hadn't been responsible about taking precautions.

"What do you plan to do?" he asked, knowing full well she would expect to get married. He knew he should offer to marry her, but he wouldn't risk leaving her a widow and his child without a father. He could offer financial support, but little more.

Silence grew between them, until her shoulders raised and lowered as she took a deep breath. Squaring them, she looked at him with a determination he'd never seen before. "It all depends."

"Depends on what?" he asked.

"On whether you can be honest."

He had a feeling he didn't want to know what that meant. "Honest about what?"

"The reason you canceled our wedding."

He couldn't tell her. Only Ernie knew what had happened to his partner in Miami, and only Ernie knew what had happened with John. Trish never needed to know about either. There was no reason to frighten her.

"I never should have asked you to marry me."

Trish merely looked at him. "That's not a reason."

He didn't remember ever feeling so uncomfortable. "I told you why."

She shook her head and turned away from him. "I still don't understand. I thought everything was good, and there was no reason why we couldn't simply postpone the wedding for a couple of months."

"I didn't mean to lead you on or hurt you. I guess I thought it would work."

She spun around and faced him, her eyes narrowed. "It would have worked."

"And if it hadn't?"

"You weren't even willing to give it a chance!"

He couldn't give it a chance, and he couldn't tell her that. He couldn't tell her what had happened to change his mind or that he still loved her.

"Failure isn't something I strive for," he finally said, hoping the discussion of the past was over. There were more important things to discuss.

"Nobody does. Honesty must be a priority in a marriage. You haven't been honest with me since I told you about the tour, have you?"

"As honest as I can be," he answered. Knowing it was the right thing to do, he did what was expected. "We should probably get married."

She lowered her head, then raised it again, meeting his gaze. "Then I'll be as honest as I can be. I've decided to raise the baby on my own," she said.

He was surprised, but at the same time, he was ashamed at the relief he felt. All he wanted was to keep her and their baby safe. "If that's what you want."

"At this point, it is."

"Am I the only one who knows?" he asked.

"No, Kate does."

"Kate?" It was just like Trish to go and tell her sister something that had nothing to do with her. Even as adults, the two seemed to live in each other's pocket. There were times it irritated him. Not many, because he honestly liked Kate, but this was definitely one of those times. "Now why did you go and tell her before telling me?"

Her head snapped up and her eyes blazed with anger. "She's my sister!"

She had kept her voice low, but fury sizzled in it, and he took a small step back. "Okay, okay. I don't know what it is about women that they have to share every little—"

"Shh," she said, glancing around the hallway. "There's no reason to shout."

He was losing his temper, something that didn't happen often. But he wasn't angry at her. He was angry at himself. "I'm not shouting," he said through gritted teeth.

"Kate and I have always shared. You know that, Morgan. You know how close we are. Like twins."

Born within less than a year of each other. And as different as night and day.

But it wasn't Kate who had him worried. It was what Agatha Clayborne might have to say. Or *do*. There was no telling how Aggie would react, and he wouldn't put it past her to show up at his door with a shotgun when she learned. Hell, it surprised him that he hadn't heard from Kate, as protective as she was of Trish.

"I'm sorry," he said, realizing he'd forgotten what it was like to be that close to someone. "Of course you told Kate."

Before he could say anything else, he heard someone in the hallway, and then Hettie appeared. "There you two are," she said, her smile reminding him of the Cheshire Cat. "I was afraid you'd both left."

He took a halfhearted look at his watch and noticed that they'd gone over the fifteen minutes he'd allotted for their little chat. "Consider me gone." Grabbing his hat and coat from the rack in the hallway, he started for the door.

"I only need a minute of your time," Hettie called out. "I need to ask—"

"Ask later." He opened the door and stepped out into the cold night. But he turned back quickly, aware that he owed them both an explanation, especially Trish. "I'm already late, and I promised Stu he could spend Christmas Eve with his wife and little boy. I'll see you both later."

He didn't bother to wait for an answer as he closed the door and hurried to the patrol car he'd parked in the driveway. After climbing into his cruiser, he started it and backed down the long driveway, his thoughts spinning.

How could he have been so foolish to have risked exactly what he had fought to keep from happening? Everything had changed fifteen minutes ago. Even if he told Trish the truth, it wouldn't help. He couldn't offer to marry her and put both a wife and a child at risk.

"MORE CAKE, Hettie?" Aggie asked.

"Maybe just a little piece. Morgan will be here soon to take me home."

"I'll make sure there's a big piece left for him."

Trish sat with the two women at the kitchen table and listened to the exchange between them, but her mind was busy with the subject of the conversation. She wished Hettie had driven herself out to the farm that afternoon to spend Christmas with them. Trish wasn't ready to face Morgan again, not after telling him the news about the baby the night before.

"What about you, Trish?"

She looked up from the paper napkin that lay in tiny pieces in front of her. "What?"

"Another piece of cake?" Hettie asked.

"No, not for me. I couldn't eat another bite." She pressed her hand to her stomach and felt a stab of guilt. She still hadn't told Aggie, and she wouldn't until she and Hettie returned from their trip. They would leave the day after New Year's. As soon as they were home again, she and Kate would tell them both their news.

Aggie pushed away from the table, her chair groaning on the linoleum floor. "I was hoping Kate would call." Glancing at the phone hanging on the wall, she shrugged. "I guess not."

Trish couldn't agree more. "She said she'd try to call today, but she didn't promise. Something about being on board and not able to call except in an emergency. But they'll be in port on New Year's Eve, so she'll probably call then."

Hettie's sigh filled the kitchen. "It's hard to believe the wedding was only a week ago."

Nodding, Trish scooped up the shredded napkin and rose from the table. "I only hope Kate isn't seasick."

"Or Dusty," Aggie added, laughing. "Wouldn't it be a hoot if a man who's spent most of his life getting bounced around on the backs of bulls were to get sick on a rocking boat?"

But Trish wasn't worried about Dusty, funny or not. With Kate pregnant, there was no telling how much of her honeymoon cruise she'd be able to enjoy. And that wasn't fair. Kate worked hard at farming and at her catering and tax businesses. She deserved the time off.

Glancing out the curtained window, Trish saw that

evening was settling in. She wasn't looking forward to encountering Morgan. Hettie had been there since early afternoon for their gift exchange, and Trish had managed to avoid seeing him when he'd dropped Hettie off at the farm. Hettie just wouldn't give up hope.

As if she'd summoned him with her thoughts, headlights flashed as a car turned into the drive and parked in front of the house. Thinking quickly, she dumped the napkin in the trash and turned to step into the hall, just as she heard a car door close. She was halfway up the stairs to her room when Hettie called to her that Morgan was at the door.

Ignoring the hint, she hurried to her room where she collapsed on the bed. She knew she couldn't hide for long. Aggie, if not Hettie, would come to fetch her to tell Hettie good-night. But just for the moment, she wanted to catch her breath. To be alone. To *not* think about Morgan or even the baby.

The reprieve lasted for only a few minutes, until she heard footsteps on the stairs outside her room. Scrambling to her feet, she grabbed a hairbrush from the nightstand next to her bed and pulled it through her hair. When the light knock sounded on the door, she was calm and ready to join the others. "I'll be right there," she called.

The door opened slightly, and Aggie poked her head into the room. "Everything okay?"

Trish pasted on a bright smile. There was no sense worrying Aggie. "Of course. I just wanted to grab—" She looked around the room and spied the present she'd bought and lovingly wrapped months ago for Morgan. Picking it up from the top of her dresser, she held it out to show her aunt, hoping that would be that.

Instead of leaving, Aggie perched on the edge of the bed. "I can only imagine how hard it is for you, seeing it's the holidays and all, and what with Kate getting married and your own plans gone awry. I just want you to know that I'm proud of you."

Tears seemed to always be just on the surface of late, and it took an effort to keep them from spilling. "I'm okay, Aunt Aggie. Really. It'll get easier. I'll feel better when Kate gets home, I'm sure."

Aggie got to her feet and laid a hand on Trish's shoulder. "Holidays are a heck of a time to have family away. A Christmas wedding sounded nice, but I don't think any of us gave any thought to them being gone during the time we want them with us the most. Now, you come on downstairs. I think Morgan has something for you, too."

Surprised that he would bother after everything that had happened, Trish gave a sniff to the tears she'd managed to hold back and followed her aunt down the stairs. In the kitchen, she found Hettie watching Morgan devour a huge piece of Christmas cake.

Looking up when they came into the room, Morgan swallowed, a sheepish smile on his face. "Nobody does this cake like Kate does," he said before taking another mouthful.

Trish crossed her arms in front of her, then glanced at Hettie and Aggie. "Kate didn't bake it."

Morgan stopped in midchew and his eyebrows went up.

"Trish did," Aggie announced.

"With a little help from Aunt Aggie," Trish added, "and a lot of notes from Kate."

"Nobody would know," Morgan replied after finishing the bite. "It's that good."

Aggie grinned, the lines in her face deepening. "We'll send a piece home with you. If you think you might want it, that is."

"I was hoping you'd say something like that."

Trish set the gift for him aside and busied herself at the sink. No one could call her domestic, although everybody seemed to think she looked the part of the perfect little wife. She tried her best. She really did. And Kate had spent an enormous amount of time teaching her the basics of cooking. At least now she could boil water without…well, without burning it and the pan. She would never be as good as her sister, but cooking a decent meal had become much easier.

Behind her, she listened to the conversation between her aunt and their guests. Everyone always felt at home in Aggie's kitchen, whether they were longtime friends or strangers. That's the way it was in the country, her aunt had told Trish and Kate when they moved in after their parents' deaths. That was definitely the way it was at the Claybornes'.

"So are you two ladies packed for your trip?" Morgan was asking.

Hettie laughed. "Packed? Are you joking?"

"You're an organized person," Morgan pointed out. "I figured your bags were sitting by the door in your apartment, waiting to be loaded into the car."

Trish heard Aggie's disgusted snort, and she smothered a giggle.

"It's a cruise, for heaven's sake," Aggie admonished. "What's to pack?"

"No off-ship adventures? No tours of the area when you dock somewhere?"

"We're docking?" Aggie asked.

That had Trish turning around, certain her aunt was joking, but by the look on her face, she knew Aggie wasn't.

"Why, of course!" Hettie cried. "Several places, to be exact."

Trish moved closer to the table where everybody was seated. "You didn't know? I thought Kate and I told you."

Aggie gave a dismissive wave of her hand, but her face showed her concern. "I suppose you did."

"You weren't paying attention."

"Maybe. Maybe not."

Hettie let out a sigh. "Oh, Aggie, it's a dream trip for both of us."

"You've been on cruises," Aggie pointed out, but didn't look her way.

"Many. But not with my best friend."

Not sure she should make things worse, but knowing her aunt needed to know, Trish spoke softly. "You'll dress for dinner on board the ship."

Aggie's eyes widened in horror. "Dress?" she croaked.

"Nothing fancy," Hettie hurried to say. "Sunday best, not black tie."

Aggie gave a decided nod, her mouth set in a firm line. "I can do that." But the worry lines between her eyes remained.

"Where will they be stopping?" Morgan asked. "I haven't heard. Don't know a thing about cruises."

Hettie turned to him. "And you from Miami!"

He shrugged and looked down at his empty plate. "Let's just say we weren't a cruising family."

"Neither were we," Aggie said, slowly sinking to her chair at the table. "Not until now, anyway."

Hettie glanced at her, and then turned back to Morgan. "We'll be stopping in Cozumel, Montego Bay and George Town."

"You'll love it, Aunt Aggie," Trish hurried to assure her. "A whole 'nother world, as they say."

Aggie grunted. "I can go to Texas for that."

Hettie pushed back her chair and stood, then grabbed Aggie's arm and tugged. "Come on. Let's go take a look at what clothes you have. I'm anticipating a shopping trip in a couple of days."

Looking up, Aggie muttered, "Heaven help me. She'll drive me crazy on a boat."

"Ship," Trish and Morgan replied in unison.

Hettie laughed as she coaxed Aggie from the room, nearly having to drag her. Trish shook her head. Her aunt had never been one for being fancy. Plain and simple, Aggie always said about herself. Trish suspected it hadn't always been that way. Her dad and mother had both mentioned more than once that in her youth, Aggie had been a beauty. Somewhere through the years, it simply had ceased being important to her.

When Morgan cleared his throat, Trish felt the need to comment. "They'll have a lovely time."

"No doubt. And probably get into some kind of scrape, knowing them. It was really nice of you and Kate to give them the cruise as a Christmas present."

Shrugging, Trish took a seat at the table and avoided meeting his gaze. "They both deserve it. Aggie has worked hard all her life. Things are better for her, now that Kate and Dusty have taken over the farming, but we wanted to do something special."

"Only you and Kate could have thought of a cruise."

She looked up, straight into his eyes. "She took in two orphaned teenage girls. She's been our mother for almost twelve years. Booking her on a cruise with her best friend doesn't come close to repaying her for everything she's done for us."

His expression was solemn as he nodded his understanding. "I know. She's one of the best. Her and Hettie."

"And your uncle Ernie," Trish added. Morgan had broken her heart, but the pieces still loved him beyond measure. She willed the thought away. She couldn't risk clouding her mind with emotions that might mean nothing to him. Not with the decisions she needed to make for her and the baby's future.

"I brought something for you," he said, getting up from the table.

"Really?" She watched as he walked to the small table by the door and picked up something hidden beneath where he'd left his coat.

"It isn't much," he said, returning with a pretty wrapped package in his hands.

"I have something for you, too," Trish said, jumping up from the table. She slipped the package from the counter where she'd left it and took it back to the table. "It's not much, either," she said, taking her seat again.

With a bit of embarrassment on both their parts, they exchanged their gifts. "Go on," Morgan urged after taking his, "open it."

Trish felt her cheeks warm even more as she carefully

began removing the tape on the ends of the package. Gently folding back the shiny silver-embossed paper, she spied the gift he'd given her. "Oh, Morgan, it's beautiful!"

"When I saw it one day when I was in Oklahoma City, I thought of you."

Tears swam in her eyes as she ran her hands over the front of the leather journal. She'd once told him that keeping a diary was something she had started as a young girl. Most of the entries had been snippets of fairy-tale stories that floated around in her mind. Those had been the beginning of her writing and what had led her to write a children's book.

"And a pen, too!" Saying too much would only make him uncomfortable, so she merely looked up at him, hoping he could see how much she loved the gift. "A very expensive pen, by the way. You shouldn't have, Morgan."

"It's only a blank book and pen."

The threatening tears vanished and she laughed. "But a beautiful blank book and a lovely pen. Inspiration to write more."

"So now I'm inspiring, huh?"

His smile was wide and relaxed, something Trish hadn't seen for a long, long time. Not since June, when everything had begun to change. If only she knew what that had been about, maybe they wouldn't be sitting at her aunt's table, exchanging Christmas gifts on one of the saddest Christmases she could remember. But Morgan had refused to discuss much of anything, no matter how often she'd tried.

"Open yours now," she urged, hoping he would like

the gift she had chosen for him, in spite of what had happened between them.

He glanced toward the door to the hallway, sudden discomfort evident in the stiff look of his shoulders. "Are you sure—"

"They're upstairs. I can hear them," she said. "Go on. Open it."

MORGAN STARED at the blue-and-gold package in his hand and wondered if the gift exchange was a good idea. He never felt comfortable getting presents. Giving was easier, even though he usually did it without much thought. In fact, there had been no thought to the one he'd found for Trish. He'd just known the minute he laid eyes on it that it was made for her.

"What is it?" he asked as he forced himself to begin the unwrapping process.

"Keep going and find out."

He glanced up to see Trish watching him, a tentative smile on her lips. Pulling a box from the wrappings, he opened it to find a set of Gary Cooper movies on DVD. "How'd you know?"

Shrugging, she stood and walked to the sink. "I guess I heard you mention once that you liked his movies."

"I love 'em." And he did. Gary Cooper was his kind of guy. As a little boy, he'd been discovered staying up late at night watching old Westerns on television, more than once. Of course he'd been immediately sent back to bed, but he suspected his mom and dad had known that he'd sneaked right back out and finished the movies, followed by dreams of being the good guy who saved the day…and the lady.

"I'm glad you like them," Trish said from where she now stood by the sink.

"They'll give me something to do on an evening when I'm off duty."

"Have Dusty put video software on your computer at the office, and you can watch to your heart's content."

He rubbed his jaw with the palm of his hand and considered the idea. Being the sheriff in Desperation wasn't time-consuming, but what would the city council think if they found out? "I'll think about it."

"More cake?"

"What? No, no thanks. But there was something I wanted to talk to you about." He hadn't wanted to, but it was something that had been bothering him since the night before, and the only way he knew to find out was to ask.

"What's that?"

"Come sit down first."

With a shrug, she joined him again at the table. She looked worried, and he sure didn't want her to be. A simple answer from her, and the subject would be closed. It was a question he was pretty sure he knew the answer to, but there was still the possibility she'd made a mistake. He only wanted to be absolutely sure.

After a quick glance at the doorway to the hall, she gave him her attention. "Go on. What is it?"

Summoning his courage, he held her gaze. "How long have you known? About the…you know."

For a fraction of a second, she stared at him, and then her chin went up, defiant and stubborn, totally unlike Trish. "Long enough."

He gathered his patience and proceeded as if it was

an interview with a stranger. "Can you explain to me what that means?"

With a sigh, she nodded. "I've suspected it for several weeks, but I wanted to be sure." She glanced toward the hallway again and dropped her voice. "I took a home pregnancy test. It was positive."

Nodding, he thought about it, although he didn't know a lot about those kinds of things. "You're sure it wasn't too early? You know, so it worked right?"

"There's no doubt, Morgan. I know my own body."

"Of course you do. I'm just trying…" Trying to what? Pretend this wasn't happening? Hoping it wasn't? That wasn't completely false, but he needed to accept this one hundred percent, without a doubt. "I guess what I am trying to find out is if you've seen a doctor yet."

"I have an appointment on Tuesday, as a matter of fact." Her chin went up again, and he suddenly saw the resemblance, plain and clear, between her, Kate and their aunt. "But there's no doubt, absolutely none."

"Okay. I just think we should make sure, before we go off making plans."

He jumped when she slammed her hands on the table and shot to her feet. "No, that isn't it at all," she said, her voice rising. "It's easier to pretend it isn't happening or to think it might be someone else's." She leaned down, peering into his eyes. "Is that it, Morgan? You think it belongs to someone else?"

"Hell, no!" he shouted back.

"That's good," she said, not moving even an inch back, "because there's never been anyone else. Not ever. Not before, not after, not ever. So if you think *that's* the way it is, you can walk right out that door right now and never—and I mean *never*—show your face here again."

"What's going on down here?"

Morgan nearly came out of his seat, sure his short-cropped hair was standing on end, and Trish had jumped up, nearly tangling herself in her chair. "Nothing. Just talking," he managed to answer as he turned to see Aggie and Hettie in the doorway. How much had they heard?

"Talking?" Aggie asked, striding into the room. "Sounded more like an argument to me."

Hettie nodded. "A loud one."

Trish sank to her chair. "It's nothing. Just a *disagreement* between two people." She slid a warning look at Morgan. "I think he's ready to go, Hettie."

He noticed that her hands, which she quickly clasped in front of her on the table, were trembling. He felt bad. Real bad. Trish would never trick him into something. He wanted to assure her that he knew that with all his heart and soul. But with Aggie and Hettie standing there, it was impossible. He knew women could be wrong about being pregnant, and he didn't want to learn, nor did he want Trish to learn, that it was a case of an imaginary pregnancy.

But he was damn glad there wasn't anyone else involved in this thing. Now all he had to do was wait until she told him what the doctor had to say. After that, he'd be ready to move forward and start making arrangements, whatever those arrangements might be.

Chapter Five

Trish sat in the waiting room flipping through the glossy pages of a magazine and wishing this first doctor visit was over. If Morgan knew that he'd put doubt in her mind, he'd be surprised. Or would he?

Frankly, she was still amazed that she'd blown up at him on Christmas Day, accusing him of thinking there was someone else in her life. She blamed her hormones. She hadn't known she could hit red rage quite so quickly. She never had before, and she was shocked by how good it had felt to let all that pent-up anger at him for the past six months surface.

She glanced at the reception desk, hoping she'd be called soon. Out of the corner of her eye, she saw the door open and the last person she wanted to see entered the room.

"What are you doing here?" she asked Morgan, unable to keep the annoyance from her harsh whisper. He took the empty seat next to her.

"Just passing by," he replied, with a nod to Cara Milton behind the receptionist's desk.

"My foot, you are." She slammed the magazine closed.

"Boring article?"

"Bad company."

One dark eyebrow raised. "I see your mood hasn't improved."

"It had," she said, hoping no one in the somewhat crowded waiting room would hear. "Are you crazy, Morgan Rule?"

"I have a right to hear what the doctor says. I have a stake in this, too."

Before she could think of a reply, Susan Fulcom, Doc Priller's nurse for as long as Trish could remember, called her name from the open hallway door of the small clinic. Trish put the magazine aside and started to stand.

"I'll be along shortly," he whispered.

She turned back to stare at him. "Morgan—"

"Don't worry. There'll be no reason for anyone to question my being here."

Although he looked sincere, and Trish didn't doubt that he had some plan to keep tongues from wagging, just the two of them speaking would raise eyebrows among Desperation's populace. And that would lead to talk. She'd hoped to keep that to a minimum, at least until she told Aunt Aggie.

With no way to point that out to him without gaining unwanted attention, she stood and walked across the waiting room to follow Susan to the examining room. Once inside with the door closed firmly behind them, she took a deep breath and let it out slowly.

"Nice to see you and Morgan being friendly," Susan said, her attention on what was probably a medical chart.

Trish froze. What should she say? Flippant answers flashed through her mind, until one that would suffice finally settled firmly. "Oh, there are no hard feelings between us."

Susan turned with a smile. "I'm glad to hear that. Maybe there'll be good news in the future?"

Oh, yes, the best of news! I'm preggers.

Trish shrugged.

"So what are you here for today, Trish?"

Trish's heart sank. She hadn't realized she'd be talking to anyone other than the doctor. How foolish had that been? Thoughts jumped in and out of her head. Susan could gossip with the best of them. Did nurses take a Hippocratic oath like doctors did? Just how long could they keep this little secret...secret?

"Why, Trish, you're pale. Lie back, honey."

Head swimming, Trish did as she was told, while Susan fussed around her, removing her shoes and generally trying to make her comfortable.

It wasn't working.

"Maybe a drink of water?" Susan asked, moving to the door.

Trish nodded, relieved to get rid of the woman while she gathered her wits.

She'd almost managed it when the door opened and in walked Morgan. Propping herself on one elbow, she straight-armed a point with her finger at him. "Out!"

Instead of obeying her command, he stood perfectly still, his eyes filled with concern. "I heard Susan say you weren't feeling well."

"I wasn't. I'm not." Lying back on the exam table, she put her arm over her eyes. "Why did you have to show up? Everybody in town will know something's up, and it will only be a matter of days before they'll have it figured out." Throwing off her arm, she popped up on her elbows. "I haven't even told Aunt Aggie yet!"

That got his feet moving, and he took the few steps to where she was half lying, half sitting, his eyes wide with what she assumed was fear of her aunt. But just as he started to say something, the door opened and Doc Priller walked into the room.

Doc looked from Trish to Morgan. "Well, hello there, young man," he said, picking up the packet of files on the small stainless-steel countertop. He gave Morgan another glance as he stepped around him and approached Trish, peering at her over the top of his rimless glasses, his blue eyes serious. "Susan tells me you aren't feeling well. What's the problem?"

"I—" She glanced at Morgan, standing silently behind the doctor. Morgan nodded.

She'd expected this to be easier. All she had to do was say she suspected she was pregnant. The words were easy. Saying them was proving not to be.

Doc turned to look at Morgan, then back at Trish. "Would you be more comfortable talking if the sheriff waited outside?"

Would she? She shook her head. "Morgan is aware of the…situation."

White eyebrows lifted, and Doc nodded, a slow, knowing nod. Reaching behind him, he pulled up a metal swivel stool and lowered himself onto it, folding his hands on the folder in his lap. "Trish, I've known you since you came to Desperation to live with your aunt. I don't judge. I don't gossip, although my wife might say different when it comes to our own family. Tell me what's going on."

"I'm pregnant." She relaxed, knowing it was over, and she felt better for having said it.

Doc's expression didn't change. "A baby is a wonderful thing. Not quite so easy when mom and dad aren't together, but still a miracle." He jerked his thumb over his shoulder and continued with, "And I take it this fella is the father?"

Trish looked past the doctor to Morgan, who was stuffing his hands into his pockets, his head down as if he was embarrassed.

"Yes, Doc."

"Then there's not a problem," Doc said, opening the folder and pulling a pen from his pocket. "He's a good man. A little stubborn maybe, but nothing wrong with that. Now you just answer my questions, and we'll have you up and out of here in no time, and no one will be the wiser." He turned to Morgan. "Have Susan step in, will you? I'll need a blood test to start with."

Trish's fears hadn't completely eased. "Will Susan—"

Doc reached out and pressed a comforting hand on her arm as Morgan left the room. "Susan Fulcom has been with me since she graduated from nursing school. She's a professional. Doesn't gossip, either, not about patients or what goes on here. If need be, we'll put our heads together and cook up an answer for anyone prying into something that isn't their business until it is. You can count on that."

Trish nodded as tears of relief stung her eyes. Wiping at them with the back of her hand, she sniffed. "Damn crying spells," she muttered.

Chuckling, the doctor leaned back. "You'll get used

to them. How's Aggie taking this news?" he asked as he began to scribble on a paper.

"I haven't told her yet."

He peered at her without raising his head, and then dropped his gaze to the paper. "I can understand your hesitancy, but I know your aunt well enough to know she'll be pleased. Maybe not so much with the circumstances as they currently are, but she'll welcome a baby with the same open heart she welcomed you and your sister."

Nodding, Trish sniffed again. "It isn't that I'm afraid to tell her. It's because I don't want her canceling her cruise on account of me," she explained. "And I know that's exactly what she'd do. I'll tell her when she gets back. I promise."

"Of course you will. Now, let's get started on those questions. Susan should be in here in just a minute with Morgan, and then we'll do the blood test. You up for that?"

Trish smiled. "That's the easy part."

He went straight to the questions with only a soft laugh to show that he understood. The questions seemed endless, starting with last date of menstruation, nausea or morning sickness, sleeping habits, loss of energy, the whole gamut. She explained about the pregnancy test, and he nodded. "Quite the thing, although not one hundred percent. It's good you came in. That's the best thing. We'll get you on a round of vitamins—"

The door opened and the nurse walked in, followed by a sober-looking Morgan. "Are you feeling better, Trish?" Susan asked. "Your color has definitely improved."

"Much better, thank you," Trish answered.

"Morgan told me the good news," Susan said.

"You'll make a great mother, Trish."

Trish could only hope so. She wasn't planning to be anything but a good mother, although she knew it wouldn't be easy. And even though she'd told Morgan she would raise the baby on her own, she knew she wouldn't be alone. She had her family and probably everyone in Desperation to help, once they knew and accepted the news.

It wasn't long before the exam was over and the blood work done, with a warning the next visit would entail more. Trish had been fine about the drawing of blood and was through it without even a wince. She'd noticed Morgan hadn't fared as well and looked a little pale.

With several papers about pregnancy and childbirth in hand, she stood at the door in the hallway leading into the waiting room. She and Morgan had agreed at Doc's suggestion that she would leave first, while Morgan waited ten or so minutes. He'd elicited a promise from her to wait for him in her car near the park.

"That wasn't so bad after all, was it?" he asked, before he pushed open the door to let her pass through.

Trish's answer was a groan. Bad? He had no idea. He'd pay for this day, one way or another. She swore he would.

MORGAN ARRIVED AT what was considered the back side of the local park, where he'd instructed Trish to wait for him. He wasn't disappointed. He could see her car as he rounded the last corner.

He wasn't sure what had gotten into her. He couldn't imagine why she'd been so riled up when he walked into the doctor's office. From the minute she'd told him the news that she was pregnant, he'd had every right to be there.

The news. He still felt a warm glow when he thought about it—right before the lead weight settled in his stomach. There was nothing to do about it now but make sure she and the baby were taken care of. He couldn't marry her, but he could do that much.

Lifting his hand in a wave as he approached her car, he watched as she rolled down her window. A bitter-cold wind blew, and he quickened his steps.

Creases between her eyes had formed as she looked up at him when he reached her car. "Was there something else we needed to discuss? Because if there isn't—"

"What are your plans for the rest of the day?"

"Stop to get some prenatal vitamins and go home, I guess. That means going to Kingfisher."

Was she afraid of the gossip? It could be tough in a small town, but she wasn't the first unmarried pregnant female in Desperation, and she wouldn't be the last. No doubt there would be some talk, but it would run its course and be done.

"I have an idea," he offered. "Where's Aggie?"

Her mouth opened and she gasped. "We can't tell Aunt Aggie! Not before she leaves."

"Not what I had in mind."

Shoulders easing, she leaned back in the seat and closed her eyes. "She and Hettie went shopping for clothes for the cruise. They don't plan to be home until well after dark."

He couldn't have asked for better. "Then here's what I was thinking. Let's go into Oklahoma City and check out the shopping malls." The pained look on her face had him quickly adding, "Only if you're up to it." When she gave a small nod, he continued. "Just for a little while. I'm not familiar with baby things, so maybe you can show me what'll be needed. I don't want you wanting for anything."

"Well…"

"We can have a late lunch afterward. Stu gave me the name of a new place. So what do you think?"

Sitting up straight, she placed her hands on the steering wheel and looked at him. "I could pick up the vitamins when we get to the city."

"Right."

"And not have to worry about someone seeing me in Kingfisher and telling tales."

He nearly pointed out that she was being paranoid, but he thought better of it. "Good idea."

"We'll take my car," she said, reaching for the ignition.

"Only if I can drive."

After making a face, she gave in. "Oh, all right. I'll follow you home and pick you up there."

Less than ten minutes later, they were on their way, the countryside flying by. "Watch your speed," Trish warned him.

He kept his eyes on the road ahead, ignoring her warning. "Nice car," he said from behind the wheel. "You made a good choice."

"I researched online and talked to people who owned one. It wasn't all that hard."

"Technology has its advantages. It drives smoother than I would have thought, and there's room in the back for passengers."

"Not to mention that the trunk is spacious and the gas mileage is good."

He was proud of her. There were some folks who thought she was nothing but a piece of fluff. Sure, she was sweet, but she was smart, too. Reasonable in most circumstances. Or so he'd thought until earlier at Doc Priller's. Sliding a look at her, he almost wished he hadn't canceled their wedding. Not that he'd had a choice in the matter.

After stopping for the vitamins she needed, they drove to the mall. Trish mentioned her fear of running into Aggie and Hettie, but Morgan thought that would be highly unlikely. Even if they did, he had no doubt Hettie would be pleased to see them together. Aggie he wasn't so sure about.

"Does a baby really need all this?" he asked, as they stood surrounded by bright colors in one of the large department stores.

"No, of course not," Trish answered. "And not at first."

He touched a fuzzy bunny hanging from the top of a crib. "Does this stuff really do anything?"

"It's stimulating." Her voice held all the patience in the world, and he paid attention while she explained. "At first they only see in shades of black and white, and then only six inches from their face. Colors and distance come along soon after."

"When do they start talking?"

"Not for a long time," she said, laughing.

It did his heart good to hear the sound of it. He'd missed it while she was gone. He'd missed it since she'd come home. If only things could be different.

So lost in thought that he hadn't noticed her move away, he wandered in the direction of where she was looking at a small cradle and talking with one of the salesclerks. Instead of joining her, something caught his eye, and he pulled a tiny football jersey from the rack.

"Cute, isn't it?"

He looked up to see a different salesclerk than the woman Trish was still talking to. "Yeah, it is."

"Is this for someone you know?"

"Not yet."

Her eyebrows went up slightly, but her smile remained. "Not here yet? I see. When is the baby due?"

"July," he answered. At least that's what Doc Priller had told them. Digging in his back pocket for his wallet, he checked to make sure Trish was still busy. "I'll take it," he told the clerk.

"I'll ring you up over there." She pointed to a counter and he followed her.

He paid for the item quickly, and Trish joined him just as the clerk handed him the sack.

"What did you buy?"

"Something."

"Well, of course it's something. What?"

"I'll show you when it's time." Taking her gently by the arm, he led her away.

"Just let me see," Trish insisted.

"Not now."

She hurried quickly beside him as he steered them through the store and out into the wide-open hallway of the mall. "Then can we go for that lunch? I'm starving."

He felt the smile coming on. "Me, too." Taking her arm, he guided her toward the exit, pleased that their shopping trip had turned out so well.

"But what if it isn't a boy?" Trish asked.

They were sitting at a small table in the restaurant

Stu had recommended, the soft murmur of the conversations of other diners all around them. It had taken some wheedling, but Trish had managed to get Morgan to show her what he'd bought in the baby department of the store. The tiny football jersey was adorable. She only hoped he wouldn't go overboard on buying things.

"Girls wear jerseys, too," he said before taking a sip of water. "Including—and especially—your sister."

She studied him for signs of his usual stubbornness and saw none. "Just so you don't have your hopes up."

"Don't worry about it."

Oh, but she would, right along with whether he would ever tell her the truth about canceling their wedding.

Filled to the brim with an excellent meal, she set her fork on her plate, dabbed the cloth napkin on her lips and leaned back in her chair to study the man she had not so long ago been engaged to. "Did you play football in school?"

"I did." He tossed his napkin to the table, but didn't look at her.

His answer surprised her. "Really? In all these years I've known you, I've never heard you mention it."

"The subject never came up."

"One more thing I didn't know about you. I mean, I know you enjoy watching football, but I never knew you'd actually played. What position?"

He looked up and stared at her across the table. "Tight end. Do you know what that means?"

She smiled as sweetly as possible. "I'm not completely clueless about sports."

"You don't. But that's okay," he hurried to say before she could defend herself. "There's no reason you should. And you can learn. If there should be a reason, that is."

She was fascinated with this. Morgan had never offered much information about himself. Not the little things, anyway. She knew he had an older sister and both a niece and a nephew. He'd grown up near Miami and had always wanted to be a cop like his grandfather. He'd had, he'd often told her, a happy childhood. Nothing out of the ordinary. She was eager to learn more.

"Were you good?"

He reached for the napkin and began to fold it. "All State my senior year."

"Wow."

"It was a long time ago, Trish." He didn't look at her. "Kid stuff."

"Our childhoods are what make us who we are today," she reminded him.

He finally met her gaze across the table. "I expect our child to have the best childhood that can be had."

"All parents do."

"I'll make sure of it. I want him or her to always feel safe," he continued as if she hadn't spoken. "That's the way it should be."

The intensity in his eyes nearly frightened her. What could have happened to have brought this on? Morgan always took things very seriously, the complete opposite of her brother-in-law. Dusty was always joking and kidding, but Kate made a point to assure Trish he had a more serious side. Morgan was totally different. It took a lot for him to loosen up. He could be very charming when he needed to be and joked with close friends. Of anyone in Desperation, except for Hettie and his uncle Ernie, she was probably the only other person who had seen the real Morgan. Usually that thought made her smile, but today it didn't. How much *didn't* she know?

"There's something I wanted to talk to you about earlier."

His voice brought her out of her thoughts and she focused on him, wondering what else was bothering him.

"What would you think about switching doctors?"

"What?" She looked around the room as if someone else had made the suggestion. "What makes you ask that?"

Leaning back in his chair, he crossed his arms on his chest. "It just seems that Doc Priller is…" He shook his head. "I'm not saying this very well."

She had no idea what he was getting at, but she had a feeling she wasn't going to like it. "I'd help, but I don't know where you're going with this."

"He's old, Trish."

"Well, of course he is," she said, her lips suddenly feeling stiff. "With age comes experience, and Doc has lots and lots of that."

"This is just another baby to him."

She stared at him, wondering if he'd lost his mind. "I bet there isn't one single baby that he's delivered in all his years that hasn't been special to him."

"He still worries me."

She couldn't believe he was doing this, but she tried to remain calm. She usually appreciated Morgan's knowledge and opinions, but this was not one of those times. "Do you have someone else in mind?"

He shook his head. "No, nobody that I know of, but I'm sure we could get some recommendations. I know some of the other sheriffs in the area. They might have some suggestions. I doubt all their wives had babies delivered by Doc Priller."

She was speechless and could only stare at him as her anger grew.

"An obstetrician here in Oklahoma City might be the best thing we could do," he continued. "You should think about it, before you get too tied into Doc."

"I don't need to think about it," she said as slowly and evenly as possible. She didn't want to ever have this conversation again. "I'm the one who's pregnant. I'm the one who's tired, whose ankles may swell to twice their size, who may yet have to deal with morning sickness. And afterward, I'm the one who'll be up for middle-of-the-night feedings."

"Yes—"

"And I say I'm just fine with Doc Priller. In fact, I wouldn't want any other doctor taking care of me and delivering this baby." She took a breath. "Is that clear?"

"As a bell."

"Good." She shoved her chair back. "Then take me home."

He got to his feet and started around the table to help her, but she was already out of her seat and heading for the exit. "I'll bring the car around while you take care of the bill," she told him over her shoulder. Somebody had to be sensible.

Chapter Six

The big, ancient stone barn behind the Commune had been converted into a community room for the use of not only those who lived at the Shadydrive Retirement Home, but anyone needing the space. The barn, which had once housed the Ravenel livestock after it was built in the early 1800s, had withstood the ravages of time as well if not better than the house had.

Tables littered the perimeter of the huge cavern of a room, where everyone waited to welcome in the new year. Champagne was at the ready as time grew nearer.

"How long?" Aggie asked.

Morgan stopped in his tracks on his way to get drink refills and turned back to look at her. "You asked that barely five minutes ago."

Trish, whose attention was on the dancers on the floor, turned to her aunt. "Until midnight? Less than an hour."

Aggie leaned across the table toward her niece, her features menacing. "That's what you said the last time I asked."

Trish leaned back in her chair, a sure sign that she wasn't willing to tangle with her aunt. "About forty minutes."

"That long?"

"Now, Aggie—" Hettie began.

"You know how I am about New Year's Eve, Hettie," Aggie said, leaning back in her chair again.

"We were eighteen," Hettie replied. "A long time ago. Let's focus on the here and now. I'm enjoying this evening tremendously."

Just as Morgan was about to turn for the bar again, Trish spoke. "What was so special about New Year's Eve when you were eighteen?"

"Just that we were finally adults," Aggie answered, "and on our own for the first time in our lives."

Morgan was more concerned with the here and now. "Do you want refills or not? I have to leave in about ten minutes."

Hettie turned in her chair to face him. "Leave? So close to the countdown?"

"I explained earlier," he reminded her patiently. "I'm on duty tonight. So is Stu. We're taking turns making sure there's no mischief going on."

"But—"

"I'll be back before midnight."

"Damn poor time to be a sheriff," Aggie commented. "Maybe you need to hire another deputy. Seems one of the two of you is always missing something."

Morgan shrugged. "That's the way it is. Somebody has to keep an eye on things." Glancing at Trish, he saw that her attention was once again on the couples dancing. He'd considered asking her for a dance earlier, but he knew she didn't want tongues wagging. He decided he wasn't going to get into an argument with her about that. Not tonight.

"Pssst."

Turning, Morgan saw Aggie looking at him and pointing toward the bar. "You better get a move on or you won't get out of here and back in time for the big blast."

With a quick nod, he hurried to finish his refill mission before leaving. "Hey, Ernie," he greeted his uncle, who took the empty glasses from him. "Why don't you let one of the other guys tend bar so you can enjoy the party?"

"I enjoy *this*," Ernie answered, filling the empties and handing them back. "I get to see everybody who's here and talk to most of them when they need a drink." He handed Morgan the last filled glass. "I see you and the Clayborne are enjoying the evening. How're things going with that?"

Guilt hit Morgan and he ducked his head to gather his thoughts. He hadn't told Ernie yet about Trish being pregnant. "Hard to avoid people you know well," he answered, raising his glass-filled hands. "Thanks."

He turned to find Desperation's city attorney headed his way. He'd liked Garrett Miles the moment he'd met him two years before, and he'd hounded the city council to hire the man. No one had been disappointed.

"Here, let me give you a hand," Garrett said, stepping up to take two of the glasses Morgan held.

"Thanks. Slopping drinks on the uniform might be frowned on by the councilmen, if not the mayor."

Garrett laughed and followed Morgan to the table where the others waited. "It'll wash."

They reached the table and passed out the refilled drinks to the ladies. Hettie took the glass Morgan indicated was hers. "Nice to see you here, Mr. Miles," she said. "Are you enjoying yourself?"

"Very much," Garrett answered, and then turned. "Hello, Mr. Mayor," he said as the man approached. "Happy New Year."

"Almost, my boy, almost." The mayor turned to Morgan. "Stu keeping an eye on things?"

"I'm about to leave to make a pass through town. Stu says everything is quiet, except for a few firecracker pops from the Grady place."

"Those kids are always up to something," the mayor joked. Placing a hand on Hettie's shoulder, he leaned down. "Stop by and see Margaret. She's almost mended from the surgery, but she needs a little company."

Hettie patted his hand. "I'll be happy to do that as soon as I get back from the cruise. You know that Aggie and I are leaving tomorrow, don't you?"

Morgan quickly glanced at his watch and didn't hear the mayor's response. He needed to be on his way. With an even quicker goodbye to the group, he hurried out to his cruiser.

Silently swearing at the way guests had parked, giving him little room to leave the makeshift parking area, Morgan was finally on his way. The town was peacefully quiet on the end-of-the-year night, and he was glad he wouldn't have to do more than drive through, checking on the places that had, in the past, been known to be trouble on such nights.

Grabbing the radio mic, he called to Stu. "Any problems?"

The radio crackled with static, as it always did, but Stu's voice was clear. "The Gradys are getting ready to set things off. I helped them make sure the garden hose was hooked up and good to go, just in case a stray cinder caused a problem."

"As damp as it's been this week, I doubt there'll be a problem with the grass, but it's good they're being careful. Head on out to the barn," Morgan told him. "I'll take care of it here and see you back at the party."

Stu thanked him, and Morgan swept down the streets, checking dark areas for movement. He even stopped by the Gradys' and wished them luck. The whole block where they lived was filling with people, eager to see the fireworks show. From past experience, Morgan knew it would be small, with only a few aerials, but neighbors loved it and so did the Gradys. Even the council turned a blind eye to the small event that bordered on illegal, according to city code.

"Hi, Morgan," Mikey Grady said, tugging on Morgan's sleeve.

Hunkering down to the six-year-old boy's level, he smiled. "Looks like you're going to have a humdinger of a show tonight."

Mikey nodded and smiled, showing off one missing tooth.

"You all be careful," he added, standing. "And have fun."

After another nod from Mikey, Morgan climbed into his cruiser and started back for the party, with only minutes to spare. At some point before the night was over, he hoped to talk to Trish about how he could help her.

"WHERE *IS* THAT BOY?" Hettie fretted. "He promised to be back before midnight. I don't want him missing out."

"He'll be here," Trish answered, pouring the champagne from the bottle they shared into the glass flutes. Morgan always kept his word. *Except once.*

"While we're waiting," Hettie said, "there's something I wanted to discuss with you."

Trish placed the bottle on the table. "What's that? And hadn't we better join the others?" She nodded in the direction of the other guests, gathering on the dance floor as they awaited the countdown to midnight. "And don't worry," she continued, knowing exactly what Hettie was about to say. "He'll join us as soon as he gets here."

Hettie didn't look convinced, but she glanced at Aggie and stood, picking up her glass. Aggie followed, and the three made their way to the center of the room. From around the dance floor, people shouted congratulations to Hettie and to Ernie for yet another wonderful party. Hettie would always be the hostess with the mostest in Desperation.

"Was there something else you wanted to talk to me about?" Trish asked as they waited the final minutes.

"I'm concerned—make that Aggie and I are concerned about you staying alone out at the farm while we're away."

Trish closed her eyes and counted to five. Hettie was worse than Aunt Aggie, always treating her like she was a child or as if she had no common sense at all. "I'll be fine," she said, as unconcerned as possible, and proceeded to check out the crowd.

"You aren't used to staying alone," Aggie pointed out.

Hettie nodded. "If you were to stay in town, I wouldn't give it another thought."

Trish turned to look at her. "Yes, you would."

"If there should be a power outage—"

"I can go into town and stay with a friend," Trish finished. "I do have friends."

Aggie wasn't to be dissuaded. "With Kate gone, I'll worry. If she was here, it would be different."

Trish took it as a personal insult that her own aunt didn't think she could manage on her own. "Why?"

Hettie jumped in immediately. "Because anything could happen. We only want you to be safe so we don't worry."

"So let me get this straight," Trish said, doing the best she could to keep from raising her voice. "If it was Kate and me at the farm alone, all would be well. Yet I can't stay there alone."

"It's the buddy system, dear," Hettie explained.

And Trish was sorely missing her buddy, especially at that moment. Kate would know how to handle this. She'd simply put her foot down and tell them both to forget it. "I don't think so."

"You don't think what?"

She turned at the sound of Morgan's voice. "I don't think they're being honest with me, that's what." She would have planted her hands on her hips, as Kate often did, if it hadn't been for the glass of champagne in her hand.

Hettie looked at the clock. "Two minutes, Morgan! Don't you think that's cutting it a bit short?"

"I made it before midnight," he answered, a mulish look on his face.

"Well, go get your champagne. It's on the table. And don't stop to talk to anyone, just get back here," Hettie called to him as he walked away. She shook her head and sighed. "I just don't know what to do about him."

"He was doing his job!" Trish cried.

Hettie backed up a step and stared at her. "My goodness, Trish. Maybe you shouldn't have that champagne, after all."

She reached for the glass but Trish held it away. "I haven't had a drop of alcohol all evening, and you know it, Hettie."

"Drink the whole thing if you want to," Hettie replied. "But do consider what we've been talking about."

Morgan, looking a little put out, joined them. "Consider what?"

Trish sighed. All she needed was Morgan siding with them. She was a big girl. She could take care of herself. Why did they have to treat her like she couldn't? She was twenty-seven years old, and it was high time she took control of her life.

"Aggie and I would like Trish to stay at my place while we're gone," Hettie explained, casting a glance at Trish as if in warning.

Trish lifted her chin and squared her shoulders to show she wasn't budging.

"We're only concerned that she'll be at the farm by herself," Aggie added. "If Kate was home it would be different."

"I can take care of myself," Trish insisted.

Hettie opened her mouth to say something, but was drowned out by revelers. "Happy New Year!" the crowd around them shouted.

Aggie looked at Hettie. "We missed it."

"We'll survive," Hettie replied.

Aggie drank her glass of champagne in one long swallow. "You don't suppose the ship will sink, do you?"

"Heavens, no!" Hettie cried. Leaning close to Trish,

Hettie put a hand on her arm. "Maybe you'll reconsider the offer?"

Staring at her, Trish opened her mouth to answer. "You two are—" she began, but she clamped her mouth shut before she said *nuts*. She also quickly reconsidered the situation. Neither of them would give up, so she would have to offer a compromise. "No, but what I'll do is promise you that if anything goes wrong or if I find I don't like being on the farm alone, I'll come here to the Commune and move into your apartment until you both return."

The worry on Hettie's face eased, and even Aggie looked a little more comfortable. "Yes. I think I can live with that," Hettie said.

Morgan cleared his throat and moved closer. "I'll even make sure of it, Hettie. And Stu and I will keep an eye on her while you're both gone."

Hettie patted his arm and smiled. "I couldn't ask for anything more. Thank you. I'll be able to leave without a qualm." She glanced at Aggie. "Well, mostly."

"Hang on," Morgan said, and disappeared into the crowd around him. He reappeared several moments later with a new bottle of champagne. Once he'd popped the cork and they'd all been spewed, he refilled Aggie's glass and topped off the others. Holding his glass high, he looked at each one of them. "A toast."

"A toast," the others repeated, holding their glasses high.

"To a wonderful cruise for Aggie and Hettie, and the best year ever for us all."

"To us all," they said in unison and finished the toast by drinking the glasses dry. All but Trish, who only took a tiny sip.

He hesitated for a moment before answering. "Right."

When she started to move away, he touched her arm. Just that small gesture reminded her of what they'd had in the past. She looked down at his hand, and he pulled it away.

"Would it be out of the question to share a dance?" he asked.

Her immediate thought was to say no, but the set of his mouth and the way he didn't look directly at her made her reconsider. "People will talk," she reminded him. He nodded and started to turn away. "But if it's just a dance between old friends," she hurried to say, "I don't see any harm in it."

He almost smiled as he held out his hand. She put hers in his and let him lead her to where several others were dancing to the slow number the DJ was playing. He turned to face her, slipped his arm around her waist, and it felt so…right. It nearly made her cry, but she gritted her teeth and told herself this was neither the time nor the place to shed tears.

She knew exactly when the other dancers spotted them. Beth Weston, Desperation's veterinarian, waved to her, her smile as friendly as always before she turned to say something to her husband, Michael. "I see Stu made it," Trish told Morgan, who held her as if she were made of fine crystal. "I'm glad he and Stacy could come."

"I sent him straight here as soon as I hit the streets. Aggie is right. Desperation could use another deputy, but whether the council will approve hiring another man…" He shrugged.

"It's worth a try though." She knew he didn't like to talk about his job. She understood most of the reasons he didn't, but sometimes she wished he would tell her how he felt about things. "I'm sure you'd have Hettie on your side."

Before he answered, the cell phone in her pocket rang. Taking it out, she checked the number. "It's Kate. I need to let Aunt Aggie know," she explained, stepping out of his arms.

She barely waited for his nod and flipped open her phone, headed for the table where she knew she'd find her aunt. "Kate?"

"It's me!" her sister greeted her on the other end. "Can you hear me?"

"Yes, but you sound kind of fuzzy."

Kate giggled. "It's just after eight in the morning. We'll be celebrating the new year in Athens tonight. Trish, it's glorious here. I wish you were here with us."

Trish laughed. "Two's company," she reminded her sister. When she reached the table where Aggie and Hettie were laughing, Morgan was still behind her.

Hettie looked up when the two of them approached. "Don't like the song?"

Trish shook her head and pointed to the phone at her ear. "It's Kate," she mouthed and returned to the call. "Why don't you talk to Aggie? She's dying to talk to you. And then you and I can have our turn."

"Whatever works best for you two," Kate answered.

Aggie stood and took the phone, moving several feet away. Hettie was watching in the low lights of the room, obviously eager to hear how the Mediterranean cruise was going.

"When you're done talking to Kate, we need to talk," Morgan said, leaning down, his voice low.

Trish heard Aggie laughing as she wondered what it might be that they needed to talk about. Things were a little better between them. He was trying, but it wasn't enough. She still needed the truth.

Aggie walked toward her, beaming. "Trish is waiting to talk to you," she told Kate, "so I'd better get off. You two keep having fun, you hear?"

Trish took the phone when Aggie handed it to her and wandered to the spot where Aggie had been. "Hey," she said into the phone.

"Trish?" Kate asked.

"It's me. It sounds like you and Dusty are having a wonderful time. So where all have you been?"

"No," Kate said, "that's not why I called. I'm so sorry I couldn't call on Christmas. Did you tell Morgan?"

Turned away from the others, she glanced over her shoulder at the mention of his name. "Yes."

"And?"

"I—" Tears stung her eyes, but she blinked them away. "I told him I couldn't marry him just because I'm pregnant."

"Was he upset?"

"Not about that. And he still refuses to tell me why he called off our wedding." The tears won out and filled her eyes, spilling over her cheeks. She knew Kate could tell she was crying and she hated that. "I'm sorry," she said, "I don't mean to—"

"Don't you worry about a few tears," Kate said, her voice stern but loving. "Tell me what's going on with you. How are you feeling?"

Trish managed to tell her about the trip to the doctor

and how Morgan had arrived and been a part of it. "I was livid," Trish said, the tears drying.

"I don't blame you. If Dusty had done something like that, I'd have given him what for."

"Oh, I did," Trish said, giving a shaky laugh at the memory.

For a moment, neither of them said anything, and then Kate spoke. "Trish, do you love him?"

With Kate, she could be honest. "Yes, fool that I am. But, Kate, I don't know how he feels about me. I know I blindsided him with the news, but he doesn't seem to have any emotional stake in this. That's what scares me. He's been this way for months, and I'm afraid this is the way he'll always be from now on."

"We'll be home in ten days, and then you and I can sit down and talk about it. Okay?"

"Yes. Okay. And…and you two have fun and don't worry about me," Trish said, wishing she hadn't dumped on her sister, raining tears on her honeymoon.

"I *will* worry, but I'll have fun, too, so don't give it another thought. I'll call you again if I get a chance, but don't bank on it."

"I won't," Trish answered, knowing her sister would do what she could. "I'll be fine. Really. Give Dusty a kiss for me, and I'll see you when you get home."

When the call ended, she made sure her tears had stopped, grateful for the low lights in the room. Hopefully, no one would notice she'd been crying.

MORGAN WAITED as patiently as he could while Trish finished the phone call with her sister. They were like two peas in a pod, but he couldn't blame them. Besides being so close in age, they'd been through and survived the death of their parents. He could only imagine the upheaval in their lives when they packed up what was left of their belongings after the tornado destroyed their home and lives, and moved in with Aggie Clayborne. From what he'd heard from others in town, there were bets on how long the girls would last under the care of an aunt who was well-respected by the community, but considered a bit odd. Women didn't farm alone. Aggie Clayborne did and was successful at it.

"I'm sorry, Morgan," Trish said as she walked toward him, "but I haven't talked to Kate since she left on her honeymoon."

"How are she and Dusty doing?"

Trish shook her head, laughing softly. "They're obviously having fun. Not that I expected there was anywhere in the world they wouldn't."

Nodding, he took her gently by the arm and led her away from what was left of the slowly dwindling crowd. "I doubted for a while that they'd get together."

"But they did, and all is well."

"You miss her."

She nodded, a sad smile on her lips. "Even throughout college we weren't apart. It's strange for her to be gone, so yes, I do miss her."

Morgan understood. He'd tried denying that he'd missed Trish when she was gone on her book tour, but the minute he saw her in her car a little more than two weeks before, he knew he'd lied to himself.

"What is it you wanted to talk about?" she asked, when they reached a storage room in the back of the old barn.

He opened the door, flipped on the light and waited while she stepped inside the room. He'd rehearsed what he had to say, knowing he'd stumble over the words if he didn't.

After closing the door behind them, he turned to her. "About what I can do to help."

"Such as?"

"Medical expenses, for one."

"I have insurance through the school."

"Then there are other things. Baby things. Whatever—" The ringing of his phone cut him off. Sighing, he answered.

"Morgan?" Stu said. "There's trouble out at the Rutgerses', and I have two cars of high school kids who think this is the night to see whose car is faster."

"Stay there," Morgan said, glancing at Trish. "I'll handle John." Ending the call, he turned to her. "I have to go. We can discuss this later."

"That's fine, I'll—"

But he was already out the door, wondering just how drunk John was this time. With red lights flashing, he made it to the Rutgerses' home in only minutes. After knocking on the door, he heard Carol, John's wife, tell him to come in.

He stepped inside, immediately checking out the situation. "What's going on here?" he asked, keeping his voice calm and steady.

John Rutgers nearly fell as he spun around and faced the sheriff.

Carol hurried to keep him from tumbling, and then looked at Morgan. "I had to," she whispered.

Morgan's heart broke at seeing the streaks of tears on the woman's face. She was still in her nightgown, her hair uncombed, her eyes red and swollen from crying. "It's all right," he told her, before directing his attention to the man who had brought all this on. "I see you've been celebrating. Lou's Place?"

"Best place to go when you need to get away," John answered, his words slurred.

Morgan shook his head, disgusted that no matter how many times he'd tried to help, John couldn't stop. "What have you been up to, John? Besides drinking again. We talked about this, remember?"

He watched as John's hands fisted at his sides. When he pulled away from his wife and tried to stand straight, he weaved back and forth so badly that Morgan went to help hold him up.

"Look at Carol," Morgan said. "Look at your wife."

"I see her! I'm not blind, ya know." But he never looked at her.

Morgan shifted to bear the majority of the man's weight and glanced at Carol. "I know you love her, John, but you're killing her. You're killing yourself. Is that what you want?"

The man turned his head slowly and looked at his wife. "'Course not." When he tried to smile at her, she put her arms around him and laid her head on his shoulder. "I just want to have a little fun, now and then, that's all," John went on, his voice becoming a whine. "She should understand that." Raising a hand, he pressed it to her hair. "You know that, don't you, sweetheart?"

Carol nodded, but said nothing.

Morgan wasn't going to let it go. "You might as well know now that I don't intend to go easy on you at your hearing. It has to stop. Now. If you pull this again, I'll make sure the judge knows everything and that you get hard jail time."

John's head bobbed up and down, and then he began to cry.

Unable to deal with the emotions of a drunk, Morgan adjusted his grip on the man. "Let's get him to bed, Carol."

It took some effort, but they finally had John in the bedroom, stripped down to his skivvies, and under the covers. "I'm thirsty," he said, done with his crying.

Morgan looked at Carol, who had turned to him for help. "Would you mind getting him a glass of water, Carol?" Morgan asked. She nodded and silently left the room. When Morgan was sure she was out of earshot, he sat on the edge of the bed. "I want you to think about how serious this is."

John nodded as his eyelids began to drift closed. He muttered something Morgan couldn't hear, but by then, Carol had returned with the water. "Just leave it on the table there," Morgan told her, indicating a night table by the bed. "You and I need to talk."

Thirty minutes later, he was on his way to the station. It took another hour to fill out the report on the incident, and he didn't leave anything out. This time John hadn't brought out his gun, but Morgan wasn't willing to give him another chance.

When the report was written, he drove by the old barn, noting that everyone had left, and then headed for home. All he wanted was some food and a few hours of sleep.

"I see you're home, safe and sound," Ernie said, when Morgan walked in the door of the Commune.

Morgan shrugged out of his leather jacket and followed Ernie to the kitchen. "John's on another binge. I had to go out there and calm him down again." Ernie turned his head to look at him, a question in his eyes, and Morgan answered it. "No trouble this time."

"There's some supper in the refrigerator. I know you didn't have any before the party." Ernie sighed and started down the hallway, pushing the swinging door open and holding it until Morgan entered the kitchen. "There should be something that can be done about him."

"There is," Morgan said, perching on one of the tall stools at the island counter. "He has a hearing later this month for drunk and disorderly. I can recommend AA or…"

Ernie pulled a covered plate from the refrigerator and put it in the microwave oven. "Jail time?"

"I don't want to do that, but if it happens again, I told him that's what I'd do. And I'd make sure the judge agreed."

"That settled him down, did it?"

"He started crying. Like a baby. Carol and I put him to bed, and then she and I talked after he'd passed out."

Grabbing the oven mitt, Ernie pulled the plate from the microwave and set it in front of Morgan. "You never put in the report after he—"

"No," Morgan said, shaking his head. "Sometimes I wish I had. Maybe he could be getting help right now."

"You were careful tonight?"

Morgan offered him a wry smile. "You've never seen me more careful. But one of these days, John is going to hurt himself. Or somebody else."

Ernie's only reply was a nod. "I'll leave you to your supper. You know where everything is."

"Thanks."

He ate his meal in the silence of the late hour. It had been close to two in the morning when he'd left the station, after filling out all the paperwork required. At least it had taken his mind off his problems. Not that he hadn't given Trish a thought, but each time she crept into his mind, he focused on the report. Now all he wanted to do was finish eating and go to bed.

Twenty minutes later, showered and in bed, he fell asleep immediately, the adrenaline rush from another ordeal with John leaving him exhausted. Dreams came and went, terrifying dreams about Trish and Carol. John with his pistol. And a small child Morgan didn't recognize.

The next thing he knew, someone was pounding on the door to his apartment. Pulled from a dream that didn't promise a happy ending, he was disoriented as fragments of it kept hammering at his conscious mind.

"I'm coming," he shouted as he threw the covers back and pulled on a pair of jeans.

"Are you okay?" Ernie asked, when Morgan opened the door.

Morgan dragged a hand through his hair as Ernie stepped inside and closed the door. "Yeah. I had...I had a dream."

Ernie studied him closely. "Must've been a doozy. Want to talk about it?"

Morgan shook his head. "It's pretty much gone from my mind."

"Well, that's good. Harold woke me. Said your hollerin' woke him and Elaine. It's a miracle nobody else heard you."

Nodding, Morgan ran both hands down his face. "I'm okay. Go on back to bed. I'll go apologize to Harold and Elaine."

"You can do it in the morning. I sent them back to bed. Are you sure you're okay?"

"Yeah. Nothing to worry about."

Ernie continued to scrutinize him, but finally shrugged. "See you in the morning, then."

"Okay."

When Ernie was gone, Morgan sank to the sofa, his head in his hands. Instead of the dream being gone, the fragments had come together. In the dream, John had somehow managed to disarm him and held a small child. The gun was pointed at the little boy's head. Morgan's little boy.

Chapter Seven

Trish, along with Hettie and Aggie, stayed behind Morgan as he cleared a path through the teeming crowd of travelers in the Will Rogers World Airport. By some miracle, they weren't late, even though Aggie had nearly backed out at the last minute. Trish was certain there would be more trouble before boarding and prayed Hettie would be able to keep Aggie calm and get her on the ship the next morning.

"We *would* have to pick the worst day of the year to travel," Aggie complained.

Morgan turned his head to look back at her. "Aggie, you're getting on that plane. And I don't want to hear that you gave Hettie any trouble at the ship."

"Or you'll what?" she asked.

"You don't want it to be known in town what a coward you are, do you?"

"Morgan," Trish warned. She was almost afraid he'd do it. She hadn't seen him since he'd hurried out on a call during the New Year's Eve party two days ago. And today he was far from being in a sunny mood.

"Don't worry, Trish. He wouldn't do that," Aggie said, continuing her argument with him.

His scowl was proof of his foul mood. "Wouldn't I?"

GET 2 BOOKS

We'd like to send you two *Harlequin American Romance*® novels absolutely free. Accepting them puts you under no obligation to purchase any more books.

HOW TO GET YOUR
2 FREE BOOKS AND 2 FREE GIFTS

1. Return the reply card today, and we'll send you two *Harlequin American Romance* novels, absolutely free! We'll even pay the postage!

2. Accepting free books places you under no obligation to buy anything, ever. Whatever you decide, the free books and gifts are yours to keep, free!

3. We hope that after receiving your free books you'll want to remain a subscriber, but the choice is yours—to continue or cancel, any time at all!

EXTRA BONUS

You'll also get two free mystery gifts! (worth about $10)

FREE!

Return this card promptly to get
2 FREE BOOKS and 2 FREE GIFTS!

HARLEQUIN®

American ★ Romance®

YES! Please send me 2 FREE *Harlequin American Romance*® novels, and 2 free mystery gifts as well. I understand I am under no obligation to purchase anything, as explained on the back of this insert.

About how many NEW paperback fiction books have you purchased in the past 3 months?

❏ 0-2
EZL3

❏ 3-6
EZMF

❏ 7 or more
EZPR

154/354 HDL

FIRST NAME

LAST NAME

ADDRESS

APT.#

CITY

STATE/PROV.

ZIP/POSTAL CODE

Visit us at:
www.ReaderService.com

▲ DETACH AND MAIL CARD TODAY! ▲

(H-AR-07/10)

If offer card is missing, write to The Reader Service, P.O. Box 1867, Buffalo, NY 14240-1867 or visit www.ReaderService.com

BUSINESS REPLY MAIL
FIRST-CLASS MAIL   PERMIT NO. 717   BUFFALO, NY

POSTAGE WILL BE PAID BY ADDRESSEE

THE READER SERVICE
PO BOX 1867
BUFFALO NY 14240-9952

NO POSTAGE
NECESSARY
IF MAILED
IN THE
UNITED STATES

Aggie slowed her steps and leaned close to Trish as Morgan continued on ahead of them. "What's his problem?"

Trish didn't have a clue, and his attitude was beginning to irritate her. "You know how he is, Aunt Aggie."

Grunting, Aggie made a face. "It's no wonder you don't want to marry him."

Trish nearly stumbled. How did her aunt know that? "I don't recall saying anything like that."

"Didn't have to," Aggie replied. "You've avoided him like the plague since you've been back."

"That doesn't mean—" Trish pressed her lips together, hoping her aunt hadn't heard her. Was she actually going to say she *did* want to marry him?

Luckily Aggie didn't notice as she continued. "Except the night before last. Care to share what that was all about?"

"Just being friendly to keep gossip at a minimum," she answered.

Hettie must have been listening. "More of that will only fuel the fire. Although I will say that it didn't look to me like it was cozy in any way. And just where did the two of you run off to?"

"We had some things to discuss." Trish tried for her most mulish expression, hoping they wouldn't continue to question her.

"Here we are," Morgan announced from several feet ahead of them, saving her from having to answer Hettie.

They'd reached the gate where they would part ways for the flight. Trish was relieved she wouldn't have to spend the next nine days under their scrutiny. She sometimes thought they already suspected something was up. It was the truth, but she'd wait to tell them after they returned home. No sense in giving her aunt an excuse to back out on the verge of their trip.

"Don't forget to call from your hotel tonight," Trish said as she hugged Hettie first. "And don't stay out all night seeing the sights in Miami. You board early tomorrow."

"Early to bed, I promise." Hettie stepped back so Trish could be enveloped in her aunt's familiar motherly embrace.

Tears stung Trish's eyes. She would miss Aunt Aggie almost as much as she missed Kate. "Please, please have a good time," she whispered.

"Hettie won't let me do otherwise," Aggie assured her. "Don't you fret about it. I'll behave myself."

Trish laughed and stepped out of her arms. "That's something I'd like to see."

Aggie frowned, and then burst out laughing. "If you talk to Kate, tell her thanks. You're right, this is a grand opportunity, and I shouldn't grouse about it. It's just—"

"I know," Trish said. "You're not used to being away from home, but I also know you'll have a wonderful time if you just relax and let it happen. That's what Kate and I want."

Morgan approached but kept his distance. "They're calling for passengers to board. You'd better get a move on, Aggie."

After Aggie had given Morgan a pat on the cheek, she and Hettie headed for the line forming at the gate, tickets and boarding passes in hand.

Trish waved and blew kisses to both women before

they ducked inside the tunnel and disappeared, while Morgan stood next to her. Feeling mixed emotions about the two women who meant the most to her being gone, she turned to Morgan, hoping her voice wouldn't betray her.

"We can leave now."

He nodded and turned back to go the way they'd come. "Is there anything you need to stop for before we head home?"

Suddenly Trish wished they'd taken two cars to the airport. She'd forgotten she'd have to share the ride home with a man in a sour mood. She longed to tell him that he should be happy. She wasn't going to tie him down to a life with a family he obviously didn't want. But she couldn't form the words.

"No, there's nowhere I need to go, except home." She could feel him watching her, but she didn't look up.

"You're sure you don't want to stay at the Commune?"

Nodding, she sighed. Were they going to get into it about that, too? "I'm positive. There's no need. I'll be fine at the farm."

"I never thought you wouldn't be."

Surprised, she tried for a smile, not completely trusting what he said.

They were well on the road home before either of them spoke again, except for some civil discussion on the traffic. It was as if they were strangers, trying to fill in the silence that separated them.

"About what we were discussing the other night..." Morgan began, and then hesitated.

It was the last thing Trish wanted to talk about. "There's plenty of time to discuss those things." Before he could say anything, she continued. "I know it was a shock to you. It certainly was to me. It still hasn't completely sunk in that I'm—that there'll be a baby in my life in only a few months. Now that Kate's wedding is over and the holidays are past, there'll be time to consider everything. Maybe once school is back in session in a few days, life will be closer to normal." At least that's what she hoped.

"I guess there are a lot of things to consider," he said, his eyes on the road ahead. He slid a quick look her way. "But you don't have to do it alone."

"Alone as in pregnant and unmarried? I will be fine." She stared at her hands folded in her lap. "Times have changed. Single women raise children without a whisper or a raised eyebrow, although it won't be like that in Desperation."

His fingers tightened on the steering wheel, so tight she could see his knuckles whiten. "Is that what's bothering you the most? What people will think?"

"What I worry the most about is Aunt Aggie. No matter what, there will be gossip."

"I wouldn't worry about Aggie. She knows how to put a stop to that sort of thing."

"She's not as tough as you think she is." Morgan hadn't seen the softer side of Aunt Aggie. How many nights had she rocked either Kate or her in her arms those first months after they'd come to live with her? Aggie's patience with her nieces had no limit. She'd taught Kate to work the farm. On Kate's demand, of course. And Aunt Aggie had done everything to make sure both girls received a college education, something she often said she regretted not having. College hadn't been a priority in her day.

"I just don't want to rush into anything, that's all," Trish explained. "I don't want either of us to regret anything."

"I won't let that happen."

Knowing he meant what he said, but that saying it didn't make it so, she let it drop. "I still have to tell Hettie, too."

Morgan had that brooding look on his face and refused to look at her. "They may not like that we aren't getting married."

"It's our decision," she replied. "They'll accept it, sooner or later."

They rode the rest of the way in total silence. She thought about asking him where he'd gone when he left the party on New Year's Eve, but knowing it was a call, she was certain he wouldn't tell her. He never had before, and he hadn't changed, except maybe to become even more secretive.

When he dropped her at the farm, she thanked him, and he reminded her to call if she needed anything. She was relieved he hadn't suggested staying at the Commune again. At least at the farm she would have the solitude she needed to think and make plans. Unless Morgan professed a desire to be involved in her life and the baby's, she suspected she was on her own.

"I'LL SEE YOU FRIDAY," Morgan said, shaking the high school principal's hand.

"We're always glad to see you," Jeff Ketcham told him. "When you're here, the whole building is as close to quiet as it gets."

Morgan laughed. "Yeah, the law seems to do that to

some people, especially the younger ones." He said goodbye and left the high school, ready for the next stop.

At the beginning of each semester he made it his job to check in with the principals of all three school buildings, high school, middle school and elementary, to schedule dates in the future to visit. Because the elementary was closer, he chose to go there next to set up the day and time for his second-semester visit.

He knew exactly where Trish's second-grade classroom was. He'd visited it often in the past, and the kids were always excited to see him. Trish always had been, too. He doubted she'd feel the same now.

He parked at the back of the building before he realized there wouldn't be a way for him to get to the office without passing Trish's room. With a shrug, he decided it didn't matter.

And that's exactly where he was when he came to a stop. From the doorway of Trish's classroom, he could see her getting the room ready for the return of her students after their winter holiday vacation. He watched as she hung colorful pictures and cutouts on the walls and remembered what it was like to be a kid returning to school after a long Christmas break. He even remembered his second-grade teacher, Mrs. Thurgood, but she wasn't anything like Trish. Did the kids know how lucky they were to have Trish for their teacher? He doubted it. Maybe they'd realize it when they grew up.

Just watching her made him long for the time before he'd canceled their wedding. Before John had gone on his worst drinking binge. John's wife had called the station that day, and Morgan had gone out to check on things. She'd been scared and crying on the phone, saying John was going to kill her. When Morgan arrived,

John was wielding a pistol and shouting at the top of his lungs. Morgan tried to calm him down, but the next thing he knew, John had him around the neck with the gun pointed at his head. Morgan hadn't been sure he'd make it out alive. And that's when he knew he couldn't marry Trish and subject her to life as a cop's wife. Bad things happened in small towns, too, just not nearly as often as they did in big cities.

While it was true that he was relieved that Trish hadn't insisted they get married, there were times when he wondered if what they were doing was the right thing. The minute he started thinking that, he reminded himself of what could happen. That stopped the wondering.

"Morgan! You scared me to death. What are you doing here?"

He didn't realize Trish had turned and seen him until she spoke. "Sorry, just on my way to set up this semester's visits."

She looked especially pretty, with a blush of surprise on her cheeks, but he suspected it was being pregnant that was the real difference he saw. She cried easily, too, he'd noticed, but he wouldn't dare point it out to her. He'd seen other changes in her as well, but he didn't think being pregnant had brought them on. She had a more independent attitude, sometimes to the point of being stubborn, since returning from her book tour, and more like her sister and aunt than he ever would have imagined. Not that it was bad, but it wasn't the Trish he knew.

"It looks good," he said, with a nod of his head toward her classroom.

Smiling, she turned and surveyed her work. "I think so, too. I hope the students like it."

"They will." When she turned back as if expecting him to say more, he decided it was time to move on. "Well, I need to check in at the office and see when they have me scheduled."

She nodded, as if dismissing him, so he turned and made his way to the school's office. "Hi, Sadie," he greeted the secretary. "Is Lorene available?"

Looking up from a stack of papers on the long counter, she flashed him a bright smile. "Hey, Morgan. Yes, she's in her office. We were just talking about when you might be dropping by."

"Can I go on in?" he asked, indicating the door to the principal's office to his right.

"Sure, sure. She's on the phone with Bill, but she won't mind."

He took the few steps to the office door and opened it wide enough to see inside. Lorene Hartman sat behind a desk piled high with papers and folders, the phone receiver at her ear. Looking up, she waved him inside. "No, Bill, get the nondiet soda. I hate that diet stuff. And tell Jenny to go with you to the store. She knows more about buying groceries than you do. Besides, she's sixteen and should be doing something besides running around town with her friends."

Morgan couldn't stop the chuckle that rumbled through him. Lorene always had a way of saying what needed to be said, no matter who she was talking to. She was straightforward and honest, but some people complained she was too much so. He didn't agree.

She groaned as she set the handset on the cradle. "Teenagers and men, the bane of my existence." Then she smiled before saying, "Now you know why I'm an elementary school principal."

"I know you love your family."

"Most days," she said with a sigh. "Today? Not so much. But I'm glad you're here. We need to go over the dates when you'll be visiting and which grades. Go ahead, make yourself comfortable while I pull the file."

He took the only empty chair in the room and waited until she was ready. He'd decided early on that it was better to meet with each grade than to try to structure a program for all ages in the school. He enjoyed visiting the kids and made excuses to stop by just to say hi.

"Here it is," Lorene announced. "You'll have to write it all down. The copier isn't working. It's like it *knows* classes start tomorrow." With a sigh of resignation, she gave him a blank piece of paper, then read the dates and times that worked best for the school and the teachers, while he jotted down the information.

Folding the paper when they finished, he put it in his back pocket. "As always, it's been a pleasure, Lorene, and tell Bill howdy for me. Jenny, too."

"If you think that'll keep her in line, you're dreaming," she said with a laugh. "But I'll tell them both. See you again in a few weeks."

He told Sadie goodbye as he passed through the office. Back in the hallway again, his cell phone rang, and he checked the caller. "What's up, Ernie?" he asked his uncle.

"Where are you?"

"At the grade school."

"Perfect. I was thinking, with Aggie gone, maybe

Trish would like some company. Why don't you stop in and ask her to come for dinner this evening."

Morgan glanced down the hallway in the direction of Trish's classroom. "Uh, I don't think that's a good idea."

"No reason she should be cooking for one," Ernie continued.

"Knowing Aggie and Kate, they froze meals for her."

"You don't have to join us, you know."

"It isn't that, Ernie. It's just…not a good idea."

"You're denying me and the others a pleasant evening with a young lady we all adore? You're a better man that that, Morgan."

Grunting, Morgan looked around to make sure no one was within hearing distance, but lowered his voice anyway. "Maybe another night."

There was a moment of silence. "What's going on?" Ernie asked.

Dread shot through Morgan. He wasn't ready to tell his uncle the news yet. Ernie would have questions he couldn't answer. Not until he and Trish could work out how they'd raise the baby apart. As far as he was concerned, it would be better if he wasn't involved. That way, there would be no emotional attachment. It was something else he needed to talk with Trish about.

"Nothing. But I talked to Trish earlier and…" He thought quickly. "She said she was calling it an early night. Getting everything ready for school to convene again tomorrow was taking it out of her."

"Oh." Ernie's disappointment was clear in his voice. "Okay. Another time, then. I don't want to keep her up late."

"Yeah," Morgan agreed with relief. "I'll be home later."

When the call ended, he felt like a condemned man who'd been pardoned at the last minute. Ernie didn't have any clue Trish was pregnant, and there was no telling what he'd have to say about it when he did.

"IF EVERYONE WILL take their seats, we'll get started on today's math lesson." Trish turned to one of the little girls in her class, who was waving her hand. "What is it, Alyssa?"

Focusing on what Alyssa was saying, Trish suddenly felt queasy. *Not again!* She took a deep breath, hoping the feeling would go away as it usually did. This was the third day she'd been sick. Until now, she hadn't had any trouble with morning sickness, and she was almost through the first trimester of her pregnancy, when morning sickness was supposed to be the worst. The past two mornings, she'd spent her free period lying down in the health room. Maybe this time it would go away, too.

But deep breathing didn't help, and she took a step back, reaching behind her for her desk to steady herself.

"Are you okay, Miss Clayborne?" Alyssa asked.

Trish braced herself against her desk and tried to nod, but her stomach decided at that moment to roll. Frantically shaking her head, she covered her mouth and ran for the door.

"She's gonna hurl," one of the boys said as she reached the door and stepped into the hallway, turning in the direction of the closest bathroom.

When she'd finally finished what she couldn't fight happening, she rinsed her mouth at the sink, hoping this would be it. She was wrong and headed immediately for the stall again. She didn't realize someone else had entered the bathroom until she opened the door of the stall and stepped out.

"Are you okay, Trish?" Chelle Trainor, the other second-grade teacher, asked. "I saw you run past my classroom door, your face as white as it is now."

"Must be a bug," Trish fibbed, wetting a paper towel to press to her face.

"It's going around," Chelle said, stepping closer. "You don't look at all good. Let's go down to the office. You need to go home, and we'll find someone to fill in for you."

Trish hated leaving school. She'd never taken a sick day, and she didn't intend to for something as paltry as morning sickness that had probably run its course for that particular morning. "I'm okay, Chelle, but thank you."

"No, you're not," Chelle said, putting an arm around her waist. "You're as white as a sheet, and you don't need to be here."

Realizing it wouldn't do any good to argue, Trish let Chelle take her down to the office. Still not feeling as well as she thought she should, she wondered if maybe she should go ahead and sign out for the day. Just this once. She couldn't let this happen again. She'd looked forward to starting the new semester after being gone since late October on her book tour. The school had been so accommodating for her, and now she might miss even more time if she didn't get this under control.

This is only the beginning. She swallowed the groan that followed the thought and wondered how long feeling this way would continue. She loved her students, and she had a job to do—a job she loved. And she meant to do it. She wouldn't let this silly morning sickness get the best of her.

By the time they stepped into the office, she'd convinced herself that she was feeling better and could finish the day. A glance at the clock told her it was an hour until lunchtime. But the thought of lunch had her stomach protesting again, and she decided she'd be skipping that.

"Oh, Trish," the school secretary cried, "you look awful." Sadie hurried around the long counter and helped Chelle get Trish into a chair. "Let me get you some water."

"No, I'm all right," Trish assured them. "I must have some kind of bug…the flu, but I'm feeling much better."

Sadie frowned as she sat in the chair next to Trish and took her hand. "Let's have the nurse take a look at you. She's over at the middle school, but I'll call and have her come here."

"There's no need, Sadie, but thank you," Trish said, wishing they would all go away and leave her alone.

Lorene came out of the office and took one look at Trish. "Go home."

"I'm feeling much better," Trish insisted, in spite of her stomach still being queasy.

"I don't care," Lorene said, shaking her head. "If it's a bug, you don't need to be passing it among the staff and students. If it isn't, you'll be back tomorrow morning, as good as new."

"I'll take her students into my room for now," Chelle said, getting ready to step out the door. "We can get a sub for this afternoon."

"But I—" Trish started to protest, but she knew she was outnumbered. She also knew her students were in good hands with Chelle already on her way to handle it. "All right. I'll go home. But I'm not happy about it."

"Good girl," Sadie said, patting her hand. She stood, but turned back. "Can you make it out to the parking lot okay?"

Trish nodded, certain she could. She had no choice in the matter. She was going home. But as she started to stand, a wave of dizziness overcame her, and she was forced to stop for a second until it vanished.

Sadie put her hands on Trish's shoulders. "You'd better sit down."

Trish tried for a laugh as she lowered herself to the chair and hoped no one would guess the real problem. "I stood up too quickly. It happens all the time."

"You can't drive home," Lorene said from the doorway of her office.

"I'll be fine," Trish insisted.

Lorene shook her head. "No. Sadie can call someone to take you home." She turned to the secretary. "Call Aggie."

Trish's heart sank. "Aggie isn't home. Neither is Kate."

"We'll find someone," Lorene assured her. "Sadie can help you down to the health room."

It was Sadie's turn to shake her head. "That's not a good idea. Jamie Braden is down there, and three others."

"She can wait in my office then," Lorene said. "There's a short sofa. Go ahead and lie down," she told Trish as Sadie helped her across the room.

After settling her on the small sofa and obviously

satisfied she was going to be all right, they left her. Leaning her head back, Trish closed her eyes. This couldn't go on.

Minutes later, Lorene returned. "We've found someone."

Trish opened her eyes. "Really? Who?"

"I called the sheriff. Stu's out sick today, but Morgan will be here in a few minutes."

Trish squeezed her eyes shut. Morgan was the last person she wanted to see.

"Is that a problem?" Lorene asked. "I mean, I know the wedding was called off, but…"

"No, it's not a problem." At least not in the way Lorene meant.

Ten minutes later, Morgan arrived. Once Trish was on her feet again, she was feeling more normal. She thanked all her colleagues and started for the door, only to have Morgan take her arm. "I'm fine, Morgan," she told him, loud enough so everyone could hear. "But we'll need to stop by my classroom so I can pick up my things," she finished as they walked out of the office.

"What's really wrong?" Morgan asked when they were only a few feet down the hall.

After making sure there was no one around to overhear, she told him, keeping her voice low, just in case. "I suspect it's morning sickness, although it's a bit late and the first time I've had a problem with it."

"Do you need to see the doctor?"

Amazed he would ask such a silly question, she looked up at him and tried not to laugh. "No, it's normal. Some women have to deal with it, others don't." That seemed to calm his fears.

When they reached her classroom, it was empty, and

she quickly grabbed her things. The two of them left the building together, headed for the parking lot. "My car's over there," she said, pointing.

"I'm taking you. No arguments."

She was halfway to her car when she felt another wave of nausea hit her, this one worse than before. At the same time, the dizziness hit again, and she stumbled.

"Okay, that's it," he announced in his I'm-taking-over voice. "I'm taking you to see Doc Priller right now."

"It's only morning sickness," she attempted to explain after dragging in a deep breath. Looking up at him, she saw true concern in his eyes. There was no reason for it. She'd be fine—just as soon as she could find out what to do to stop it.

Chapter Eight

"Right in here, Trish." Fran Simpson, the doctor's other nurse, showed Trish and Morgan into the room. "Kick your shoes off, Trish, and lie back. If you'll push your sleeve up, I'll check your blood pressure to make sure everything's okay with it."

"She was as white as a bleached sheet in the school office," Morgan said as Fran wrapped the cuff around Trish's upper arm. He didn't think he'd been so scared since John had pulled the gun on him. His nightmare rated only second to that.

"Have you been having any morning sickness?" Fran asked Trish.

Trish nodded as the cuff tightened on her arm. "I've had a couple of episodes of feeling a little squeamish, but nothing quite this bad until this morning."

With the stethoscope at her ears, Fran merely nodded. She finished, moved it to hang around her neck and pulled the cuff from Trish's arm. "Your blood pressure is perfect," she said with a smile. "That's always good news. Just make yourself comfortable, and the doctor will be with you in a few minutes."

"I don't know how anybody could be comfortable on these exam tables," Trish grumbled when the nurse was gone. "And now there's one more person to worry about letting something slip."

"Fran wouldn't do that," Morgan assured her, more worried about her and the baby than town gossip.

"I hope not."

The door opened and the doctor stepped in, followed by an attractive dark-haired woman who appeared to be in her late twenties. "Back so soon, Trish?" Doc asked as he skimmed a file.

"Afraid so," she answered, glancing at the woman.

"Trish is one of our second-grade teachers," he told the woman. "And I guess I should introduce you all." He placed his hand on the woman's shoulder. "This is Dr. Paige Miles. Paige, this is Trish Clayborne. I'm sure you'll be meeting her aunt Aggie when she returns from her cruise. And Kate, her sister, when she's back from her honeymoon."

Dr. Miles smiled at Trish and offered her hand. "It's very nice to meet you."

"Miles?" Morgan asked. "Any relation to our city attorney?"

"Garrett is my brother," she explained, turning to Morgan. "He kept telling me how great Desperation is, and I decided to see for myself."

"Morgan Rule is our sheriff," Doc said in introduction. "Paige will be taking over for me in the next few weeks."

"Oh, Doc, you're not leaving us!" Trish cried.

He patted her arm. "It's time to pass the care of this town on to someone younger. I've been doctoring here for almost fifty years. And Barbara has been nagging me to take it easy and do some traveling."

Trish glanced at Morgan, and it was all he could do

to keep from gloating. He'd been right. Doc was getting too old.

"We're all going to miss you," Trish told the doctor. "Aunt Aggie isn't going to be happy, either."

Doc laughed. "Aggie Clayborne is as stubborn as they come, but she's a good woman." He turned to Dr. Miles. "You keep that in mind. She'll argue with you until you're blue in the face, but she'll do what she's told to do. Most of the time."

Paige's brown eyes twinkled. "She sounds like fun."

Morgan snorted. "That's one way of putting it."

"Morgan!" Trish shook her head, warning him to be quiet.

"I'm kidding," he said. "Aggie's a peach."

"Let's get back to you, Trish," Doc Priller said. "I want you to know that Paige will be the one delivering this baby of yours. I can keep treating you up until my official retirement in March, but after that, she'll be taking care of you."

"Whatever works best," Trish said, smiling at the new doctor.

"Best would be that I take over now," Dr. Miles explained.

"I'm fine with that."

"It's all settled, then," Doc Priller announced. "I'll have the files changed. What seems to be the problem today?"

Trish shot a warning look at Morgan, and he remained silent, more than willing to let her do the telling. "I've been feeling great," she answered. "No morning sickness until a couple of days ago, but it wasn't bad. Then this morning I nearly lost my breakfast in front of my students and was feeling dizzy."

"Probably nothing at all to worry about," Dr. Miles said to both Morgan and Trish. "Blood pressure is good, and considering she's still in the first trimester, there's nothing unusual with a little dizziness accompanying the nausea, especially on an empty stomach."

"So what you're saying is—" Morgan began.

"I don't see anything to worry about," Dr. Miles finished, turning to Trish. "One trick is to keep a little something on your stomach to keep the queasies away. Crackers, cookies, whatever works. Midmorning can be the worst, so keep a package of something in your desk drawer. A small snack might be all it will take. If not, try a little milk or even some herbal tea with the snack."

Trish looked past the doctor and flashed Morgan an I-told-you-so smile. "I'll be sure to do that."

"But if it should get to be too much to handle, come back in. We can run a few tests, just to make sure, and there are meds I can prescribe if needed."

Morgan didn't understand any of this. "If that's the case, why not do the tests now?"

"She's the doctor," Trish reminded him. "If she says later is better, then it is."

Feeling he was outnumbered, Morgan held up his hands. "Okay." But he would still worry, especially with Trish staying alone at the farm.

"As for the dizziness," the doctor was telling Trish, "I'm convinced it's only because of the empty stomach and probably low blood sugar. The snack should take care of that, too, but just in case, try to keep from standing in one place for long periods. I'm sure that sounds impossible when you're teaching, but you can use your desk for support. Also, take it easy when you stand from a sitting position. Slow and easy, when at all possible."

Trish nodded.

"Do we need to make another appointment for you?"

"I was in last week," Trish answered, "and set it up then."

Dr. Miles nodded. "Good. And we'll do a full exam then, unless there's a reason we need to do one sooner." She glanced at Morgan as she said, "But that's highly unlikely. I expect the morning sickness will be short-lived. You're a healthy young woman, so I don't foresee any problems."

"Thank you, Dr. Miles."

"Oh, please. Call me Paige."

As the doctor and patient chatted, Morgan could see a friendship blossoming between the two of them. It wouldn't hurt if Trish found a new friend. Kate would be busy with a new husband and might not have the time to spend with her. And having her doctor as a friend would ease his mind, as far as her health and the health of their baby were concerned. If Paige Miles was as good at doctoring as her brother was at the law, Desperation was lucky to get her.

"I'll see you in about three weeks, then," Paige was saying, "but if you have any more concerns, call or come in."

"We will," Morgan answered and meant it. Feeling a little better about the situation, he started for the door. "I'll meet you out in the waiting room, Trish."

She nodded, but her attention was on the doctor. "I

hope my sister, Kate, will come to see you when she gets back from her honeymoon cruise. She's expecting, too."

Morgan stopped in his tracks. "Kate's pregnant, too?"

"Really?" Paige asked at the same time. "What a great thing for the babies to be so close in age."

Trish turned to Morgan. "Keep quiet about it, okay?"

Nodding, he eased out of the room, wondering why Trish hadn't mentioned Kate's condition before. But Aggie hadn't said a word, so he was fairly certain she didn't know, either.

In the hallway, he met Doc Priller, who stopped him. "Don't worry about her, Sheriff. She comes from strong stock. Oh, she may look delicate, but she's as strong as her aunt and her sister."

"Sometimes I forget that," Morgan admitted. "And I worry." He wouldn't tell Doc how much. The images in his dream hadn't left him.

"I know she's worried about people talking," the doctor continued. "They will. In Desperation, that's something you can count on. But it'll pass. It always does."

"That's what I'm thinking," Morgan agreed. "We'll all be sorry to see you go," he added sincerely.

"What do you think of Paige Miles?"

"She'll do okay. I guess you could say she has a good bedside manner."

"That she does. I hope she stays on here for a long time." The doctor moved away. "I have patients waiting, but you keep in mind what I said about Trish. Give her some space, and she'll do the right thing."

As the doctor moved on to another patient, Morgan knew that's what he planned to do in the future. He would give her all the space she needed. And more. But was he willing—

He shook his head. He couldn't even consider what was going through his mind.

TRISH STEPPED INTO the reception area and spied Morgan talking to one of the councilmen. When he saw her, he ended the conversation and waited at the door for her. "Ready to go?" he asked.

She nodded as she joined him. "Can we pick up my car at the school first?"

Pushing open the door, he waited for her to step outside, and then followed. "You aren't thinking of going back to your classroom, are you?"

"No," she answered and noticed his relief. "I only hope this is short-lived. I don't want to have to miss school another day."

She climbed into the cruiser and he shut the door, then circled around to the driver's side and slid in. He was silent as he pulled the car away from the curb, causing Trish to wonder if something was bothering him. She knew better than to ask. There had been many times in the past when she had wished he would open up more, but he rarely did, and she had eventually adjusted to that. Now she wondered if maybe she should have insisted they talk more.

"I don't suppose you'd reconsider staying in Hettie's apartment," he said. It was more a question than a statement.

She didn't even need to think about it. "No."

"I'm going to worry if you stay out at the farm, what with the dizzy spells."

He would, she knew, and she didn't want to give him anything more to worry about. But she wasn't willing to spend close to a week in the same building where he lived.

"I'm serious about this, Trish," he went on. "There's always someone around at the Commune, in case you need help or aren't feeling well. You can always say you have some kind of bug that's going around, and no one will know about the baby."

She doubted that. Some women seemed to have a sixth sense about those things. She'd wondered on Christmas Eve if Freda might be one of them. "I'll say it one more time. I'll be fine."

"You're serious, aren't you?" he asked.

"Yes, I am." When she saw his jaw harden, she knew an explanation was in order. "As you said that first night I came home from the tour, we can be friendly with each other, but avoidance would be best."

"That's not what I said."

"Close enough." But she remembered that he had used the word *avoid*. He probably did, too, but he wasn't going to admit it. It was plain to see that he wasn't happy, but she was more concerned with her own happiness. Yes, it was selfish, but it wouldn't be long until the baby's needs would come first. She needed to grab some "me" time before that happened.

When she looked out the window, she realized they weren't headed for the school. "Where are we going?"

"I'm taking you to the farm."

"You don't need to do that," she protested. "I can drive myself."

"I'll bring your car later and have Stu take me back to the office," he continued.

"It's not necessary."

"I won't stay." He glanced at her, and then focused again on the road ahead as he drove out of town. "Look, I promised Hettie and Aggie that I'd look after you while they're gone. Breaking that promise would get me in a lot of hot water." After another quick glance, he shook his head. "I should be taking you to the Commune."

Crossing her arms, she said nothing.

"I don't want you lifting anything, or doing things you know you shouldn't. Let me know, and either Stu or I will help."

She could tell by the hard set of his jaw that it wouldn't be wise to argue. Not this time. It might lead to a stay at the Commune, and she just didn't want that to happen. "All right," she said, sighing.

"And don't—"

"Morgan, for pity's sake," she said, her exasperation nearly overwhelming her, "I'm not a teenager. I can take care of myself."

"Right," he said, but he didn't sound convinced.

She couldn't understand what all the fuss was about. She was experiencing some rather natural morning sickness. The idea of staying alone at the farm for a few days didn't bother her. After all, it hadn't been that long since she'd spent six weeks in hotels and had survived. A week at the farm would be a piece of cake.

When they arrived at the farm, she was feeling fine. But as she climbed out of the cruiser, her stomach began to feel a bit uneasy, and she decided it was time to give Paige's advice about a little snack a try.

"I can let myself in," she told Morgan when he got

out of the cruiser and followed her. "You can go on back to work."

"Are you sure?" he asked.

"Very sure."

He nodded, and then looked directly into her eyes. "You're sure you're going to be okay? I don't relish the idea of having Hettie and Aggie mad at me for not keeping my promise to them."

"You don't need to worry."

He didn't say anything for several seconds, just looked at her. "You'll let me know if you need anything or start feeling worse?"

"I promise I will." She crossed her heart with a finger and smiled.

She tried not to watch as he pulled away and headed back to town. There were so many things she loved about Morgan. He was always thoughtful and never missed an opportunity to make certain she was comfortable. He didn't rattle on about things she wasn't interested in, not sports, not his work, not anything. At least that's the way it had been before early summer. And the last few days, he'd been acting even more strange. Maybe someday he would open up and tell her what he was thinking.

At least that's what she hoped as she let herself into the kitchen and headed straight for the cookie jar.

"ERNIE?" Morgan called, opening the door to his uncle's rooms in the Commune.

When there was no answer, he sat on the sofa and relaxed as much as he could. His thoughts turned to Trish as they always did. She had always been close to his uncle. Ernie was a good man, and Morgan reminded himself of how lucky he was that his uncle had chosen

Desperation as the place to settle down. Most everyone in town liked Ernie, and Hettie had taken to him immediately, or so he'd been told. The Commune had been Ernie's idea, and Hettie had been all for it, eagerly helping to get it started and pleased that the place had done so well under his management. If it hadn't been for his uncle, Morgan wasn't sure where he'd be now. He'd always be grateful Ernie had taken him in when he'd been looking for sanctuary from the tragedy that had caused him to leave his job in Miami.

In the midst of his mind's rambling, his uncle walked in. "You're home early," Ernie said.

"I'll go back later. Stu isn't feeling so great, so I'll take his late shift after I get some supper."

"Stu's sick?" Ernie asked. "I heard you took Trish to the doctor's office from school."

Morgan realized it was time to let his uncle in on the secret he'd been keeping. "Maybe you'd better sit down."

Ernie's eyebrows shot up as he settled on his favorite chair. "Okay, what's going on?"

Morgan took a deep breath. The best way to do this was to just jump right in and say it. "Trish isn't sick."

"No?"

"No." For some reason, Morgan was having a problem getting the words out.

Rubbing his short-cropped beard, Ernie appeared to be unconcerned. "It's none of my business, but Hettie mentioned she'd offered her apartment to Trish while she's gone. I don't have a problem with that. After all, this whole place is hers. And Trish doesn't need to be staying out on that farm by herself."

"She's pregnant," Morgan blurted.

Ernie looked him square in the eye. "Your baby?"

Morgan nodded.

"Well, that changes the color of everything, doesn't it?"

Morgan nodded. "Color, size, you name it." He could feel his uncle watching him, but he couldn't look at him.

"How long have you known?"

"Since Christmas Eve."

"That long?" Ernie asked. "Why didn't you say something?"

Shaking his head, Morgan sighed and sank to one of the chairs. "I don't know. I just…"

"You what?"

Morgan shook his head again and looked at the floor, his hands clasped between his knees. "I don't know."

Shifting in his chair, Ernie cleared his throat. "You'll have to explain that."

"She's doesn't want to get married."

"Give her some time."

Morgan looked up. "That's what Doc Priller said. The crazy thing is she's more concerned about gossip than anything."

"There'll be gossip, no matter what you two do. It's inevitable in a small town. And after canceling the wedding…"

"I know," Morgan said, nodding. But could he tell his uncle the truth? That he agreed that marriage wasn't the answer?

"Things are different now than they were twenty years ago. Women have babies and raise them on their own. Gossip will die down. It has before. I'm sure Trish knows that."

"She's more worried about how Aggie will take the gossip," Morgan explained, battling his own indecision about what was best.

"Aggie knows?"

"No," Morgan admitted. "Trish didn't want to tell her before the cruise. She was afraid Aggie would cancel the trip."

"Hettie would have, too," Ernie agreed. "While I don't think keeping something like this from them is a good idea, Trish did the right thing."

Morgan agreed. But could he do the right thing? As far as Aggie was concerned, Morgan knew she wouldn't come after him with a shotgun or force either of them to marry when they didn't want to.

"Have you called home and told the family?" Ernie asked.

"Why would I do that?"

Ernie sighed. "I know you're a grown man, but your mom and dad will want to know they're going to be grandparents."

"They already are," Morgan pointed out.

"Those are Jen's kids. Do you think because your sister has two kids that your mom isn't going to be thrilled to know you'll have one?"

"I hadn't really given it any thought. There's been so much going on," Morgan admitted.

"There's the phone," Ernie said, pointing at his desk. "Give them a call."

Morgan wasn't ready to do it. What could he tell them? That he was relieved Trish wasn't going to marry him? How would he explain that? "I'll do it later."

"Do you want me to call them?"

"No, no, I'll do it, but… I think you should know something else."

Ernie leaned forward, concern in his eyes. "What?"

"I agree that Trish and I shouldn't get married." He watched Ernie's face, hoping to see a reaction that said his uncle understood.

Getting to his feet, Ernie walked to the other side of the room, and then turned around. "I'd have to agree that if both parents aren't willing, then marriage isn't the answer. And if Trish wants to raise the child on her own, I have no doubt she can do it. But is that really what you want?"

"After what happened in Miami with Ben and seeing how it affected Connie, yes," Morgan answered, ignoring the doubts he'd been having. "I broke off with Trish for that very reason."

Ernie was silent for several seconds. "Which was a mistake."

"Not as far as I'm concerned."

Shaking his head, Ernie returned to his chair. He rubbed his hand down his face and sighed. "You've got to let the past go, Morgan. You'll never move forward in your life if you don't."

Morgan agreed only partially. "Maybe I could have, if it hadn't been for John." He considered telling his uncle about his dream, but decided against it. Ernie would insist it was nothing more than a simple nightmare, caused by stress. Maybe it was, but Morgan had seen it more as a prophecy. A warning. "I told her I'd help out financially."

"Is that it? You'll give her child support?"

"Pretty much, yes."

"What about being a father?"

As much as he knew it would hurt to give up a relationship with his child, he had to. "I can't let an attachment be formed."

"You're leaving town, then?"

Morgan stared at him. "What? No! Why would I leave Desperation? It's my home, as much for me as it is for you."

"Then how do you think you'll manage to keep away from your own child?" Ernie asked, leaning forward in his chair. "Don't you think everyone will know the baby is yours?"

Even that was something he'd considered. "They might not."

"How?"

"Trish could've gotten pregnant while she was away." He knew it was a reach, but it might be a possibility, depending on how things were handled.

"You don't believe that, Morgan. You can't. And I don't believe you'd even want that. Now call your mom and give her the news, then I want you to talk to Trish and get this worked out with her. Everything. I don't imagine she's going to let you get away with ignoring your own child."

Morgan wasn't sure she would, either, but he didn't know any other way to handle it. He'd miss so much, he knew, if he wouldn't allow himself be a real father. If there was another way he could do it and still keep them from possibly coming to harm in the future, he'd do it, but there wasn't.

"I'll call her later, when everything is worked out."

Ernie stood, looked at him and walked to the door. Opening it, he turned back. "Good luck with working it out."

Chapter Nine

"I can't believe they did this," Trish muttered on her way to the Commune. "And it isn't going to stop when I tell them I'm pregnant. They'll insist that Morgan and I get married."

When she realized she was driving down the street alone, and was talking only to herself, she laughed. Leave it to Hettie and Aunt Aggie to get her riled up.

She had no doubt they'd collaborated on this scheme of theirs. She had stopped in at the office during her lunch hour to talk to Lorene about school things, and Sadie had given her a note—a message from her aunt. Aunt Aggie and Hettie were on their way home and asked if she'd meet them at the Commune as soon as the school day was over. Ernie was picking them up at the airport, and they weren't certain what time they would be arriving.

"I should have known they'd do something," she said, then laughed again. At least the baby would be well-accustomed to her voice if she kept this up.

Pulling into the drive at the Commune, she noted Ernie's car wasn't there. "It figures." Getting out of her car, she smiled at her new idiosyncrasy and walked up the stone steps of the building.

She wasn't surprised to see Morgan standing in the hallway when she opened the door and walked inside. "I knew they'd find a way to make sure you were here, too."

"You did okay at the farm by yourself, I take it," he said.

"I've been fine all week. The advice Paige gave me did the trick."

He nodded, but it was as if he hadn't heard her. "We never did finish that conversation about finances. I'd like for you to make up a list of what you expect they might be."

She couldn't believe he was still at that, when she'd told him there was no hurry. The morning sickness might be gone, but her temper wasn't. "I swear, Morgan, you just want to make things more complicated than they—"

"We're back!"

Trish spun around to see her aunt and Hettie coming in the door and rushed to give them both welcoming hugs. "I didn't expect you two until later," Trish said as she followed them into the Commune's kitchen.

"Our flight was early and Ernie made good time," Hettie replied, plunking her carry-on onto an empty chair.

"And we come home to find you two arguing," Aggie added. "What is it this time?"

"Nothing," Trish answered.

Morgan glared at her. "She's being stubborn, as usual."

Aggie walked over and touched Trish's cheek. "Ernie said you'd had a short bout with the flu or something. Are you feeling okay now?"

Wondering just how much Ernie knew, Trish nodded. "I'm fine. It was nothing."

"I need to get back to work," Morgan announced, and was gone from the room before anyone could comment.

"Seems Morgan isn't so pleased to see us," Hettie said, when the sound of the front door slamming was heard.

"Stu's been sick," Trish explained.

"Caught your bug, did he?" Aggie asked.

Shrugging, Trish didn't want to dwell on the subject. She hated lying, and that's what she'd been doing for weeks. She was relieved she wouldn't have to continue with the deception much longer. Kate would be home in a few days, and together they would share their news.

Ernie walked into the kitchen with a suitcase in each hand. "That boy needs some time off," he said, setting the bags on the floor.

"Just one more reason they should hire another deputy," Hettie replied.

"Don't hold your breath," Trish muttered.

Aggie looked at her. "Sounds like someone else could use some time off, too."

Trish tried for a smile and a shrug. "First week back after the holidays is always hectic with the students. They're starting to settle back into the routine again. I guess we all are."

"Ernie," Hettie said, with a wave of her hand, "just leave the luggage there. Right now, all I want to do is sit down and put my feet up. You'd think sitting in an airplane and an airport for hours on end would have me wanting to run a race, but all I want is to go up to my apartment and sleep in my own bed until morning."

"But we did have a good time talking to those soldiers in the airport," Aggie added.

"Soldiers?" Trish asked, looking from one to the other.

"Oh, yes," Hettie answered. "They were nice young men and were happy to sit and talk with us."

"And just how many of them were there?" Trish asked, imagining her aunt and Hettie surrounded by a battalion of twentysomething men in uniform.

Hettie smiled at Aggie before answering. "Only three, dear, and they were very well-behaved."

"Probably more behaved than we were," Aggie added with a laugh.

"You should have been there with us," Hettie added. "Maybe we could have hooked you up."

Trish didn't mean to gasp, but she couldn't believe Hettie was talking that way. "Well, thank you very much, but I don't need to be 'hooking up' with anyone right now."

"Why's that?" Hettie asked, looking like the cat that had just eaten a big, big mouse.

"Because I—" Trish shook her head. "Never mind." She turned to her aunt. "If Hettie is going to call it an early night, maybe we should be getting home."

Aggie frowned. "It isn't even five o'clock," she said, giving her friend a scowl. "I don't know what's wrong with her," she said, jerking her thumb at her friend, "but I'm wide-awake and ready to go again."

Trish couldn't help but feel smug. For someone who hadn't been excited about taking a cruise, it was plain to see that Aggie had enjoyed herself. "That good, huh?" she asked.

Aggie fought a smile, but finally laughed. "So you

and your sister were right. We had a wonderful time, and I thank you for the gift from the bottom of my withered old heart."

Trish reached to give her a hug. "I'm so glad, and I know Kate will be thrilled."

"Speaking of Kate," Aggie said, returning the hug and then stepping back, "didn't their cruise end today?"

"Yesterday," Trish answered. "But she said they might take a day or two to see the sights in New York City."

"Even better," Aggie said, chuckling. "The sights are probably getting a kick out of Dusty."

"Maybe," Hettie said, her eyes sparkling with mischief, "he could get together with that singing cowboy, and they could do a duet. You know, the one who stands on the corner in the all-together with his guitar."

Just imagining her brother-in-law in anything other than blue jeans and a T-shirt with boots—or less—had Trish laughing, which sent Aggie and Hettie on to more absurd things and into gales of laughter.

"I thought you said you were tired, Hettie," Aggie said as she wiped tears from her eyes.

Having a difficult time catching her breath, Hettie nodded. "I am. And that's why...I find it so...funny."

Trish managed to compose herself and tugged at her aunt's arm. "Come on, Aunt Aggie. Let's allow Hettie to get some rest. Maybe we can plan an evening of reminiscing tomorrow for the two of you. I can't wait to hear about your trip."

"And the soldiers, too, I'm sure," Hettie said, hiccuping, which started her laughing again. With a wave of her hand, she shooed them away. "Go on, both of you. It's going to take me an hour to settle down."

Ernie had disappeared and returned. "I left all of your

luggage and packages by Trish's car," he told Aggie, and then turned to Trish. "Are you sure there's room in that car of yours?" he asked as he followed her and Aggie out the door. "What with Aggie's suitcases and all."

"Oh, sure there is," Aggie answered. "I don't have that much."

But Trish wasn't so certain. "I didn't know I'd be picking you up, and I have several boxes from school in the car that I need to take home."

"We'll manage," Aggie assured her.

Trish's uncertainty proved to be initially correct, but they discovered that by shifting everything around several times, they were able to get everything inside the car.

"A gnat wouldn't find a place to light in here," Aggie said from the passenger seat.

"We're fine," Trish assured her, "although I wouldn't want to take a cross-country trip squeezed in like this."

With a wave to Ernie, Trish pulled away from the Commune, glad to have her aunt home again. Aggie seemed to be lost in her own thoughts, and Trish's wandered over the past few days and the upcoming ones.

"So what's been going on in Desperation while we were gone?" Aggie asked.

The question not only brought Trish back to the present, it also made her cringe inwardly with guilt. As far as she knew, there weren't any rumors or gossip going around, except that Morgan had driven her to the doctor's office when she'd become ill at school. Even that had died down quickly, and she still had hope that nothing would surface before Kate was home and they had a chance to tell Aunt Aggie.

"Trish?"

Trish jumped at the sound of her aunt's voice. "Sorry."

"Woolgathering, were you?" Aggie asked. "Well, I guess we both were. I can tell you for certain that I'm feeling a bit like Hettie and can't wait to sleep in my own bed, in my own house. We'll have a bite to eat, and then I'm going to bed."

"That sounds good," Trish agreed as she maneuvered the car around the last turn before getting to the farm. She'd enjoyed her days spent alone, but there had been times she'd been lonely. It would be good to have Aggie there to keep her company. Mentally crossing her fingers that Kate would be home soon, she decided that acting normal would be the key to avoiding any suspicion that something was going on.

THE COMMUNE WAS QUIET the next morning when Morgan walked in the door. He could hear some of the residents talking in the dining room, but he didn't stop to say hello. Stu was feeling better and had shown up for work, insisting that Morgan take a few hours and get some rest. Morgan was grateful. He'd been up most of the night before catching up on paperwork, and then all night again. Luckily, Desperation had been quiet.

He made his way slowly up the stairs, unable to hurry because he was bone weary from too little sleep. Finally making it to the door of his apartment, he opened it and stepped inside to a silence he'd been craving for days. He wouldn't sleep long. A couple of hours would refresh him until later that night.

He was pulling off his shirt when his cell phone rang. When he picked it up and checked the caller's number, he smiled. He hadn't heard from Connie, his former partner's wife, for several months. With two kids to take care of, he knew she was busy and left it to her to initiate keeping in touch.

"Connie! To what do I owe this pleasure?"

Her laugh was refreshing and he was glad to hear it after all she'd been through. "I know I'm late with the holiday greetings," she began, "but merry Christmas and happy New Year, Morgan."

"To you, too," he answered, glad that she had called and not just sent a note in the mail. "And the kids? How are they?"

"They're good. I meant to send you some pictures, but we've been so busy, what with the holidays and all. Ben played football this fall. And he's driving! He'll be graduating this coming spring."

Morgan shook his head, unable to believe Ben's son was that old. He'd missed so much after leaving Miami. "Little B.J. graduating. Time sure does fly."

"We're hoping you can make it down for his graduation ceremony."

Morgan thought of the boy he'd last seen almost six years ago. Connie sometimes sent photos, but it wasn't the same. "I wouldn't miss it," he said. "And Tasha? How's she doing?"

Connie laughed. "She's in love."

Morgan couldn't believe it. He could accept the younger Ben growing up, but not Tasha. "But she's only—"

"Fourteen, Morgan. It's a crush—or at least I hope it is—but he's a nice boy from a nice family, so I don't worry. Not too much, anyway."

"I don't know how you do it, Connie, on your own

and everything." He wondered how Trish would handle the same task. At least she wouldn't have to worry about money.

There was a brief pause before she spoke again. "That's another reason why I called. I'm getting married in May."

Morgan couldn't think of a time when he'd been more surprised. "Married?" he asked. "Connie, are you sure? I mean, it's only been—"

"It's been six years, Morgan. A long time, especially when you're alone."

"It doesn't seem that long." But it was, and he knew it. He'd stayed in Miami for six months after Ben was shot and killed. The department had insisted he take a leave of absence until he'd dealt with what had happened. He'd spent that six months helping Connie and the kids. In turn, they'd helped him see that he didn't belong in Miami anymore.

Connie's voice brought him out of the past and back to the present. "Sometimes it seems like a lifetime."

Morgan still couldn't make sense of it. "But after Ben was shot you said—"

"I know," she answered, her voice filled with the emotion of those months after Ben was gone. "I didn't think I could go on. Not ever. It was hard those first couple of years without Ben there. After you left was the hardest. You helped me so much, Morgan. And then my family helped. But all that still didn't fill the hole inside me. And then Mark came along and, well, life began to get better. I began to live again, feel again, and it wasn't just hurt I felt any longer."

"Mark?" Morgan asked.

"Mark Basinger."

Morgan stopped breathing. He must have heard wrong. He knew Mark Basinger, had shared a beer with him several times at department socials and picnics and whatnot. It wasn't that he didn't like the man. Mark was an okay guy, but—

"You're marrying another cop?" he blurted into the phone.

"Ironic, isn't it?"

As if it was almost funny? A joke? But Morgan knew it wasn't. "I can't believe—" He stopped, ashamed that he'd said what he was thinking and corrected himself. "I'm surprised you'd do that again."

"I never thought I could, but I've learned a lot of things in six years."

"But you and Ben…I mean, you loved him so much," Morgan reminded her. "I've never known two people who were so perfect together."

He heard a sigh, and then she said, "I still love him. I always will. But the time came to move on. I don't think Ben minds. In fact, sometimes I think he's been pushing me along. And believe me, Mark was as resistant as I was."

"So he wasn't coming on to you?"

"No, he never did that," she said. "Not ever. He was just there, a friend when I needed one. And then it became more as time went on."

Morgan still couldn't wrap his mind around Connie putting herself and her kids back in the same position where she'd been before. Not after what had happened. She'd been devastated when Ben was shot, on the verge of taking her own life, if it hadn't been for B.J. and Tasha.

"Are you sure?" he asked. She'd be dealing with the same things again. Those things they'd talked about, like always wondering if she'd get a phone call that something had happened, that Ben had been hurt or even killed. The memory of that night flashed through his mind. "I couldn't do anything about it," he said, not realizing he had said it aloud.

"It wasn't your fault, Morgan. There wasn't any way you could have done any more than you did. You know that. I know that." She sighed again, and when she spoke, her voice was softer. "Ben knows that. I'm a stronger woman for it. I've healed. And life goes on. It has to. Ben would want it to."

"I just can't…" Morgan tried. "It's hard for me to understand."

"Then let me tell you what I've learned," Connie went on, her voice stronger. "I loved Ben with all my heart. He was a good man, a good father, and an unbelievable husband. I'm thankful for the years we had together. He'll always live in my heart. But loving a dead man isn't healthy. The kids needed someone who would look out for them and love them the way their father did. They felt the emptiness, too. I'm a lucky woman. I've not only had the love of one special man, but I now have the love of another."

Confused, Morgan didn't know what to say. If he hadn't spent time with Ben and Connie and seen the special bond between them, he might be able to accept what she was saying. But it was her choice, and he had no right to question it. "If that's what you want, Connie."

"It is. But what about you? The last I heard, you were engaged. Are you married now?"

He heard the hope in her voice and hated to disappoint her, but he couldn't lie, either. "No. I called it off."

"Why? What happened?"

He hesitated telling her, then decided it was only right that she know. "I couldn't risk putting her through what you went through. She's too good to have that happen to her."

"It sounds like you still love her."

"I do. I can't stop."

"Then you're a fool if you don't get down on your knees and beg her to marry you. And I never thought you were a fool, Morgan Rule. Not ever."

He decided not to tell her about the baby. It wouldn't change anything. Connie's life might be turning out better than anyone would have expected, but he wasn't convinced Trish's would in the same situation.

"I just can't do that to her, Connie."

The silence from Connie was unnerving, but she finally spoke. "Okay," she said, the disappointment in her voice evident. "I can see that talking to you won't make you see, so I won't try. I still hope you'll come down for Ben's graduation."

"I will," Morgan promised. "Just tell me where and when, and I'll be there."

He wrote down the information she gave him and then the call ended. Sitting on the sofa, his boots and shirt off, wearing only his socks and jeans, he'd never been more confused.

Sure, Connie had found a way to go on with her life, and he suspected Trish would, too, if the same happened to her. But he didn't want to test it. He'd seen what Connie had gone through. He'd held her in his arms and calmed her, while she grieved over Ben's death. She'd said life would never be the same. For him, that was true. It never would be.

Six years had gone by like a speeding car. Ben's kids had grown up. They were teenagers now, not children. He didn't want to miss seeing his own child grow up. Was he willing to risk being a part of that child's life? Did he have a choice?

Chapter Ten

"Trish, could you take that ham out of the oven?"

Ready to head out the door for a long walk in the crisp January afternoon, Trish set her journal and pen on the table and grabbed the oven mitts. "Sure thing, Aunt Aggie. What time did you say Hettie would be here?"

"In about an hour," Aggie called from the hallway. "If I could just find that recipe of Kate's for her sweet potato casserole…"

Trish opened the oven door and leaned over to grasp the big roaster. "The recipe book is in the drawer by the phone," she said, easing the roaster toward her on the oven rack.

"Why didn't I look there first?" Aggie asked, now standing in the doorway.

Trish grinned as she pulled the roaster from the oven and placed it on top of the stove. "Because it was the most likely place for it, maybe?"

Aggie gave an unladylike snort. "And it's always in the last place you look."

"I should think so. Why keep looking after you've found it?"

Aggie pulled the handwritten cookbook from the

drawer and thumbed through it on her way to the table. Settling on her usual chair, she pushed her new eyeglasses higher on her nose and stared at the open book in front of her. "Yes, indeedy."

Trish didn't know if she was talking about the recipe or her comment, but she didn't ask. "Do you need me for anything else?"

Aggie looked at her over the top of her glasses. "Are you going somewhere?"

"Just out for walk." Trish grabbed her journal and pen from the table. "You found the recipe?"

"I'm sure this is it," Aggie said, stabbing the page with her finger. "At least I hope so."

"What if Kate and Dusty don't get here until late? She said they had one stop to make before they'd be home."

Shrugging, Aggie stood, the cookbook in hand, and crossed to the small pantry closet. "We'll have ham sandwiches, if it's that late. I just hope I can do this recipe proud."

"I'm sure you can. I'm the one who can't cook."

Aggie glowered at her. "That isn't so, and you know it. Not anymore."

"Thanks to you and Kate." Her mind spun at the thought of what she would soon be doing. She was looking forward to her sister's return, but she also knew it meant she couldn't put off telling Aggie about the baby. Moving toward the door, she stopped. "I think I heard a car door shut."

Aggie dropped the cookbook on the counter and hurried to the window by the door. "I can't see who it is."

Footsteps sounded on the wooden porch, then the

door opened wide. "We're home!" Kate announced and stepped into the kitchen.

Being closest to the door, Aggie grabbed her in a hug first. "So you are." Holding her at arm's length, she looked Kate over. "How'd you get that tan?"

"It was hard work," Kate said, laughing.

"It was a lot of time on deck," Dusty, walking in behind her, announced. "Not to mention those nude beaches."

After giving her new brother-in-law a playful punch in the arm for his joke, Trish took Aggie's place and hugged Kate. "It's so good to have you home again," she said, her voice filled with emotion, while tears of happiness appeared in her eyes.

"It's good to be home," Kate answered. Stepping out of the embrace, she smiled. "You're looking healthy."

Trish could read the question in her eyes. "Feeling healthy, too," she assured her.

"Sit down, sit down," Aggie told them after returning to her seat at the table. "I'll get a crick in my neck looking up at you all."

Dusty and Kate laughed as they pulled out chairs and joined Aggie at the table. Trish moved to sit across from them, admiring their tans and happy smiles. "Tell us all about the cruise."

"Oh, it was marvelous!" Kate said, nearly bouncing out of her chair. "The water was so blue it was almost like looking at the sky. I couldn't tell where one ended and the other began. But how was your cruise, Aunt Aggie? I haven't talked to you since before you left on it."

"Be honest, Aunt Aggie," Trish whispered loud enough for all to hear.

Aggie looked from Kate to Dusty, a frown on her face. "You really want to know?"

Kate nodded while Dusty said, "Of course we do."

Her expression still solemn, Aggie answered. "Well, I'll tell you. It was—" She stopped and a grin spread across her face. "Wonderful! I've never had so much fun in my life."

Everyone started talking at once, and Trish sat back in her chair, enjoying the stories they shared and compared. She hadn't been sure the cruise for Aggie was a good idea when Kate had first suggested it, but now she had to agree that it had done their aunt wonders.

"No seasickness?" Kate asked.

"A little pinch that first day," Aggie answered with a shrug. "But after that? Not a bit. How about you?"

Kate opened her mouth to answer, but Trish saw Dusty put a hand on Kate's arm. "She's a real sailor," he announced.

Trish suspected whatever seasickness Kate had experienced was more morning sickness than anything else.

Aggie harrumphed. "And I suppose you didn't feel a twinge," she said, eyeing Dusty.

"Oh, a little. We had a couple of days when the seas were pretty rough, but it wasn't bad."

Trish flashed her aunt an I-told-you-so look, remembering how Aggie had predicted he'd be standing at the railing most of the trip. Aggie acknowledged it with a tiny shrug and grin.

"We have tons and tons of pictures," Kate said.

Aggie put her palms on the table and pushed herself to her feet. "And I have sweet potato casserole to make."

"I can help," Kate said, standing.

"No, you won't, missy," Aggie ordered. "I said I'd do it and I will. But don't be too disappointed if it doesn't turn out as good as yours."

"Then that *is* baked ham I smell," Dusty announced, sniffing the air. "How soon do we eat?"

The three women looked at each other and laughed. "You'll never change, will you, Dusty?" Trish asked, loving to tease him as much as everyone did.

"Nope. And now that I'm married, I expect my waistline will prove it." He patted his big belt buckle and licked his lips, darting a glance at his new wife.

Aggie crossed to the stove. "If you want a taste of that ham and the rest, you'd better get out of my way. I like to do my cooking alone."

"So how soon are we going to eat?" Dusty asked again.

Aggie snorted with laughter, while Kate and Trish looked at each other and giggled. "In about an hour," Aggie finally answered. "Hettie will be joining us."

Kate looked from Trish to Aggie. "Morgan, too?"

"Morgan's working the late shift," Trish answered.

Kate's eyebrows raised slightly, questioning.

"Hettie mentioned it," Trish explained.

Dusty sauntered to the door and grabbed the hat he'd left on the counter. "Well, if it's going to be that long, I'm going to run this luggage home."

"I'll go with you," Kate said, moving to join him.

"No, you stay here with Trish," Dusty told her. "I'm sure you have a lot to talk about." Winking at Kate, Dusty opened the door. "I'll be back in time to eat, don't you worry."

"Oh, we'd never worry about that," Kate said.

When he was gone, Aggie waved a large wooden spoon at the two girls. "Out of here, both of you."

"Let's go," Kate said, giving Trish a playful shove. "If we don't, she might smack us with that spoon."

Laughing, the sisters ducked into the hall and up the stairs. Once they were in Trish's bedroom, Kate collapsed on the bed. "It seems like forever since I've been in this room."

"And it's only been a few weeks," Trish answered, sitting on the edge of the bed.

Kate propped herself on her elbows and looked at Trish. "You haven't told her, have you?"

Trish shook her head. "I wanted to wait until you were home. But you haven't, either," she reminded her.

"You're right," Kate said, "so why don't I tell her first?"

"Maybe I should go first," Trish said. "You can then step in to save me before she smacks me with that wooden spoon."

Kate fell back on the bed, laughing. "*That* brings back memories."

Trish nodded, giggling. "Like the time you talked me into making mud pies, and we used up all the seasonings and herbs—"

"And then actually tried to bake them in the oven."

"On broil," Trish added, unable to keep from laughing. "There was mud all over the inside of the oven."

"Every time I see that spoon, I remember the paddling we got for it."

"We deserved it."

Kate nodded. "We did. Aunt Aggie has never been unfair." Sitting up, she reached out and held Trish's hand. "Are you still of a mind not to marry Morgan?"

"I've thought long and hard, even before I came back from the tour. It's for the best." Trish looked at her sister and saw the concern in Kate's eyes. "He's offered to help financially. I only need to decide how we'll do that."

"I'm sure you'll work it out. But is that really what you want?"

Nodding, Trish felt tears sting her eyes. "At this point, yes."

"You don't think marriage would be better?"

She turned to stare out the window where the bare branches of the tree swayed in the winter wind. "Not unless something changes." She looked back at her sister. "Not unless Morgan changes, and only he can do that."

"I don't understand," Kate said. "I know he's been moody and was even before you told him about your tour. And I have to say that I don't think his reason for calling off the wedding had anything to do with that, but that's just my opinion."

"I don't think it did, either." Shaking her head, Trish sighed. "I can't marry him, Kate, and I get the feeling that's the way he wants it."

"Why?"

Trish shrugged. "He's only talked about money, nothing else. I'm not even sure he wants to be a part of the baby's life."

Kate reached over and took her hand. "I can't imagine anyone, even Morgan, doing that. He'll come to his senses."

"To be honest, if he doesn't, I'm okay with it. I guess we'll have to see what the future brings." And if it brought a life without Morgan in it, she would love their baby twice as much.

MORGAN ROLLED the cold beer bottle between the palms of his hands and thought about Connie's phone call. He could accept that she'd found someone to share her life with, and he was happy for her. But why another cop? It didn't make sense.

Glancing up from the table where he sat in Lou's Place, he saw Dusty walk into the tavern. Dusty acknowledged him by raising a hand in a hello, to which Morgan replied with a nod. *The age-old sign language of men.* He suspected Dusty knew Trish was pregnant, but he wondered who would be the first to bring up the subject. Morgan smiled as Trish's brother-in-law walked toward him. The smile was genuine, but his thoughts were at odds with each other.

"Have a seat, if you'd like," Morgan said, inclining his head toward the chair across the table from him.

"Thanks." Dusty took the seat and settled onto it, eyeing the bottle in Morgan's hands. "Drinking on duty?"

"What?" Then Morgan realized what he meant. "Not on duty. See?" He pointed at his shirt. "No badge."

"Ah. I didn't notice. Trish said you were working late."

Morgan nodded, not knowing what to say. When Hettie had badgered him about taking her out to the Clayborne farm to welcome Dusty and Kate home from their honeymoon, the lie came easily. He wasn't in the mood for a family get-together. At least not until he could sort through the things that had been bothering him.

Morgan suspected Dusty would understand and decided to tell him the truth about working late. "I guess I could say that plans changed."

"You could," Dusty agreed.

"But we both know better."

Dusty flashed him an understanding smile. "Hettie?"

With a sigh, Morgan nodded. "It was the only way to keep her from insisting that I should be there."

Shaking his head, Dusty chuckled. "Hettie and Aggie. I don't know any two people more…"

"Conniving?"

"That would be the word."

"I know they mean well, but…"

"They do," Dusty agreed, "but that doesn't mean they can't both be royal pains at times." He waited while the newest waitress took his order for a cold beer, then tipped back his hat with one knuckle and grinned. "You might rethink that invitation, though. Aggie baked a ham and was starting a sweet potato casserole when I left. It should be ready within the hour."

It was Morgan's turn to chuckle. "Now if you'd said Kate had baked the ham and was making the sweet potatoes, I'd bet you I could make it there faster than you could."

"I don't know. Aggie can bake a mean ham."

"So how was the honeymoon?" Morgan asked.

Dusty laughed before answering, and then waited as the waitress brought his beer and walked away. "I'd be crazy if I said it was awful. It was great. Kate got to see places even I've never seen, and I've done more than my share of traveling. A once-in-a-lifetime experience, even if Kate wasn't feeling up to doing a lot of sightseeing at first."

"She was sick?"

Dusty looked down at the bottle in front of him. "Sort of."

"That kind of sick, huh?"

Dusty laughed. "Yeah, that kind. I guess Trish mentioned that."

"Briefly."

Dusty shook his head. "Those two sisters tell each other everything."

Morgan was about to get the answer to his earlier question. "So you know—" He didn't have to finish. Dusty merely nodded. "I should've figured that." Needing to change the subject, he said, "I doubt I could ever afford a trip like the two of you took."

Dusty leaned forward. "Something I learned along the way, and a short way, at that, considering. It doesn't matter where it is, as long as you're together."

"I guess you're right," Morgan said. "But I'll probably never know."

"I was going to ask if everything is okay, but I guess you just answered that question. I don't know where you are with this, but I know where I was. I didn't want a wife. Rodeo was all I needed. I found out I was wrong. Admitting it was hard, but it was worth it."

Without thinking, Morgan said what he was thinking. "Trish doesn't want to get married."

"And you agree?"

Morgan nodded, and then shook his head. "It's kind of complicated."

"You've talked to her?"

"As much as she'll let me. She doesn't seem to want to listen."

Dusty grunted and tipped back in his chair, but he

kept his voice low when he spoke. "It must run in the family. Kate had her mind made up that she was going to be a single woman, just like her Aunt Aggie. She probably still would be if I hadn't made her listen. Once I figured out what *I* wanted, that is."

Morgan couldn't keep from laughing. "I remember that well. Fourth of July celebration, and you roped and tied her in front of half the county after you chased her through town."

"Yeah," Dusty said with a low chuckle, "it took tying her up to keep her still. I tried it without the rope, but it just wasn't working. Sometimes you've got to take the bull by the horns." He settled the chair on all four legs and leaned forward. "Those Clayborne women are a stubborn bunch."

"You're telling me? And Trish has always been so sweet-natured." Morgan shook his head. "Lately, she's like Jekyll and Hyde."

"Hormones," Dusty muttered. "And then there's the fact that you canceled the wedding."

Morgan couldn't make eye contact. "I had my reasons."

Dusty leaned closer. "Does Trish know that?"

"It's not something I can talk about."

After checking his watch and taking another drink of beer, Dusty stood and laid a ten-dollar bill on the table. "Beer's on me. I'd better scoot. Don't want to miss that baked ham." He started to turn away, but hesitated. "Look, I won't pry, but I will tell you this. You can't keep secrets from those women. If you try, you'll regret it."

Morgan could only hope he was wrong. Telling Trish

about what had happened in Miami and the incident with John wouldn't change anything.

Or would it?

"As soon as these sweet potatoes are done, we'll eat," Aggie announced.

Hettie, sitting at the table with a cup of coffee, looked up as Trish and Kate walked into the kitchen. "There you are!" She got to her feet and hurried to give Kate a hug. "You look great!"

"Yeah?" Kate asked, laughing. "I feel pretty good."

Hettie's smile was wicked. "So you enjoyed your honeymoon on the high seas?"

"I didn't have a choice. It was unbelievable."

Hettie released her, and Trish watched the exchange, her heartbeat speeding up as she thought about what was coming. It was probably a good thing Hettie had joined them. She and Kate could tell them both at the same time. Double trouble if it didn't go well, but her hopes were high it would.

The timer went off, distracting Trish and announcing that supper was almost ready. "Are we eating in here?" she asked.

"Don't we always?" Aggie asked, taking the casserole from the oven.

"I just thought that with Kate and Dusty home, we might want to eat in the dining room."

"The kitchen is fine with me," Kate chimed in.

"Dusty's gonna miss this if he doesn't get here soon," Aggie grumbled.

Kate glanced at Trish and nodded. "He'll be here. But before he does…" She gave Trish an encouraging smile. "You might want to sit down, Aunt Aggie."

The two older women looked at each other, then Aggie shrugged and took her place at the head of the table. Both of them looked worried.

"Is something wrong?" Hettie asked, getting right to the point.

Kate smiled. "Well, *I* don't think so, but I'll leave that up to the two of you to decide."

Aggie turned to look at Trish. "You already know about whatever this is?"

Trish nodded and tried to hide her own smile.

"Well, not all of it," Kate corrected. When no one spoke, she said, "I have news."

"News?" Hettie asked, her frown deepening "What kind of news?"

Kate turned to smile at Trish, and Trish nodded. Facing her aunt and Hettie, Kate announced, "I'm pregnant."

For several seconds, neither of the two older women said anything. "Really?" Aggie finally asked.

Kate giggled. "Really."

"That was quick," Hettie said, looking a bit stunned, but happy, if the smile on her face was any indication.

"Oh, Hettie," Aggie said, "nobody counts months anymore. Come here, girl," she told Kate.

"Of course they don't," Hettie replied and got to her feet to wait her turn to give Kate a hug.

"A baby," Aggie said, as if the idea was just sinking in

"Well, not exactly," Kate said, laughing.

Hettie didn't even get her hug before stepping back to look at her. "And just what does that mean?"

Kate turned to flash a grin at Trish, who had no idea what else Kate might have to tell them.

"Twins."

Trish stared at her sister. "Twins? Oh, Kate!" And then she started laughing. "I can't believe it! You stinker. You didn't tell me."

"I only learned this afternoon," Kate explained. "That's the stop we had to make. We had a wonderful time on the cruise, but I was sick for a few days, and Dusty made me promise to see Doc Priller as soon as we got into town."

"You met Paige?" Trish asked.

"Oh, yes," Kate cried, "and she's wonderful. She was sure she heard two heartbeats, so she did a sonogram right then and there. There was no question about it after that."

"Unbelievable," Trish said, and then hugged her sister, laughing. "This is wonderful news!"

"When are the babies due?" Hettie asked. "Oh, I can't believe it's *babies!*"

"Mid-August."

Hettie and Aggie settled at the table once again, still talking as if they'd had a hand in it.

"Help me set the table," Kate said to Trish. "Dusty will probably be here soon."

Trish knew that was her cue to share her own news. Her hands shook as she mindlessly pulled silverware from the drawer. She'd expected this to be much easier than it had been with Morgan, but—

"Trish has news, too," Kate said, matter-of-factly, as she took plates to the table.

"What's that?" Aggie asked, looking up at Kate.

Hettie leaned forward, a wide smile lighting her eyes. "Is the wedding on again?"

Trish hated to disappoint Hettie, but she hoped her news would make a difference. "I'm pregnant, too."

Aggie looked at Kate and then back at her. "Both of you?"

Trish nodded when Kate did, and then the tears fell. "Why are you crying?" Aggie asked, reaching out for her. "You come here and sit down."

Trish complied. If only she could stop crying!

Kate giggled. "I get the morning sickness, she gets the weepies. What a pair we are."

Aggie looked at Hettie. "I think Trish had a bit of that morning sickness." She turned to Trish and took her hand. "Was that what that bug was?"

Trish could only nod and sniff.

"Three babies!" Hettie said, hurrying to give her a hug. "Oh, Trish, there's nothing to cry about. Babies are a blessing."

"I know," Trish managed.

Aggie squeezed her hand. "And when should we expect this one? Hettie and I will have to go on a shopping spree."

"Middle of July."

"Why, they're almost triplets," Hettie announced. "And, yes, a shopping spree—several of them—are called for." She rubbed her hands together. "Oh, I can't wait!"

"Could be more twins," Aggie said with a wink.

Trish laughed, finally getting her emotions in order. "No! Just one. I hope."

"You can count on Paige checking on that," Kate said, sitting next to her. "Won't it be great? Both of us?"

Trish nodded, unable to speak as she saw the love and excitement in everyone's eyes.

Aggie got her attention again with another squeeze of her hand. "You weren't afraid to tell me, were you?"

Trish thought about it and decided to be honest. "A little. At first."

"Well, that's just foolishness. These things happen all the time," Aggie said, glancing at Hettie.

"They do," Hettie agreed with a nod. "I'm guessing Morgan knows?"

"Since Christmas Eve," Trish answered.

Next to her, Aggie gasped. "You've known since then? Both of you?"

Kate nodded, and so did Trish.

"Why didn't you tell us?"

"And give you a reason not to go on your cruise?" Kate asked. "No way were we going to let that happen."

Trish was surprised to see her aunt blush. "Well," Aggie stammered, "you have a point there. So I'm glad you waited."

Hettie picked up her cup, stood and went to the coffeemaker. "I'm going to ask the question we're all thinking of asking but haven't," she said as she poured another cup of coffee. "Are you and Morgan planning to get married?"

Before Trish could answer, Kate did. "There's a bit of a problem with that."

Hettie's eyes widened as she returned to her seat. "What? He hasn't asked? If I get my hands—"

"No," Trish said quickly. "I made the decision not to get married."

"You don't want to marry him?"

Trish wasn't sure how to explain. "No, I don't. I have…reservations."

"You don't have to marry him," Aggie said, patting her arm. "Not unless Kate gets her hands on that shotgun."

Trish could only smile. Explaining wasn't easy.

"Go on, Trish," Hettie said. "Nobody here is going to judge you."

Nodding as she realized this was her family, and she could tell them anything, she folded her hands on the table. "It's just that he's not the same man as the one who proposed to me almost a year ago. Something happened. I don't know what, but he's changed."

Hettie nodded. "He has. Sometime back in June? I don't remember for certain."

"You noticed it, too?" Trish asked.

"He… I don't know. He just kind of pulled into himself."

"Before I learned about the book tour and told him about it."

Aggie let go of Trish's hand and stood. "Well, it doesn't matter. It was foolish of him to call off the wedding. I didn't think he was a fool, but I've been wrong before." When everyone stared at her, she stared back. "Well, I have. It's your decision, Trish, and no matter what, we're here for you. We can plan a wedding or we can change diapers. It makes no difference to me."

"That goes for all of us," Hettie chimed in. "Times have changed. It's so much more acceptable than it was in our day to keep a baby if you weren't married."

"Just ask Hettie," Aggie said, getting up from the table. She suddenly stopped, a stricken look on her face.

"It's all right, Aggie," Hettie told her. Turning to the

girls, she sighed, then smiled. "There are things you don't know."

Trish looked at Kate, who looked back at her. "Like what?"

Hettie hesitated before answering. "I gave up a baby for adoption, years and years ago."

"Oh, Hettie," Trish cried and hurried to her side.

Kate moved to kneel beside Hettie. "That had to be hard. However did you manage to get through it?"

Hettie's smile was sad for only a moment. "Aggie helped me through it. I don't know how I could've dealt with it all, if it hadn't been for her."

"That's what friends are for," Aggie said, returning to her seat with her coffee. Hettie reached over and squeezed her hand, and Aggie winked at her.

"Can you—" Kate began, but didn't finish.

"Talk about it?" Hettie asked. "Of course I can. Aggie and I went to Chicago after we graduated from high school."

Kate raised her eyebrows at Trish. They'd known there was something about Chicago in Aggie's history, but nothing else.

"We— I met someone. A young man who had just joined the army. We fell in love and, well, things happened. By the time I knew I was pregnant, he was serving in Vietnam. I couldn't go home. In those days, people in Desperation weren't so broad-minded, and I knew my news wouldn't be welcomed by my father. I was young and scared and alone, except for Aggie." Her smile for her best friend was filled with gratitude, and she took a deep breath before continuing. "And I didn't have a way to tell Will. The best thing was to relinquish my baby to be raised by two parents who would love her and take care of her."

The kitchen was quiet as each of them thought of what Hettie had been through. Trish was certain they all were wondering what had happened afterward. "You know it was a girl?" she asked.

"Oh, yes," Hettie answered. "In fact, you've met her daughter. Do you remember the young girl who came to stay with me several years ago?"

Trish nodded.

"She was a couple of years younger than me," Kate said. "Didn't she date Boone Randall while she was here?"

Hettie nodded. "Yes, she did. She's my granddaughter. Her mother didn't know she was here, but it was such a joy to have her with me, if even for a little while. Now you know why I'm so glad the times have changed."

The door opened and Dusty stepped inside. "Is the food ready?" he asked, rubbing his hands together and eyeing the table. "What?" he asked when they all looked at him. "A man has to eat."

All four women burst into laughter. "Oh, Dusty," Kate said, going to slip her arms around his neck. "Your timing is, as always, perfect."

The table was quickly loaded with ham, sweet potato casserole and green beans from the garden. Talk turned to spring and a summer filled with babies. Trish joined in, but her mind was busy. Looking around the table, she knew she could count on the people dearest to her. She also thought maybe someday Morgan would tell her what had happened in his life to make him change his mind about marrying her.

Chapter Eleven

It was late when Morgan let himself in the front door of the Commune. After Dusty had left him at Lou's Place with some things to think about, he'd ordered a sandwich and concentrated on what he needed to do. That would have been easier if he'd known what he *wanted* to do. He didn't.

As he started up the stairs to his apartment, he heard someone close one of the doors down the hall. He stopped, suspecting it was Ernie. He was right.

"Come on into my office," his uncle said when he saw him. "We need to talk."

Tired, Morgan hesitated. "Can we do whatever this is tomorrow? It's been a long day."

Ernie peered at him over the banister. "Whatever you think," he said with a shrug and then turned to start back down the hall. "But you might find it interesting."

"Okay," Morgan answered, but even he heard the frustration behind the word. Ernie wouldn't bother him about anything that wasn't important, so he followed him down the hallway to the Commune's office. "What are you doing up so late?"

Ernie opened the door and stepped inside. "Hettie wanted me to tell you something."

Morgan followed, but stopped just inside. Hettie was probably still angry that he hadn't joined her at the Claybornes' for Dusty and Kate's welcome-home dinner. Pulling off his hat, he raked his hands through his hair. "I don't need to hear Hettie's latest lecture, even if it's watered down through you."

He turned and put his hand on the doorknob, ready to leave, until his uncle spoke. "I think you need to know about this."

Morgan looked over his shoulder and saw that his uncle was serious. "Okay, what is it?"

"Hettie knows Trish is pregnant, and so does Aggie."

Releasing the doorknob, Morgan faced his uncle. "Is that supposed to be good or bad?"

"Don't ask me," Ernie said, raising his hands in surrender. "But she wanted you to know."

Morgan nodded, relieved that Trish had told her aunt. "I'm glad they know. Maybe they can talk some sense into Trish. She doesn't seem to want to talk about the expenses."

He turned again for the door, but Ernie hadn't finished. "Maybe somebody should talk some sense into *you*."

This time, Morgan jerked his head around to stare at his uncle. "I'm the only one acting like a rational adult about this. For some reason, Trish doesn't want to include me on this. I just want to make it easier for her to provide for the baby."

"Is that all you plan to do?" Ernie asked.

Morgan shrugged. This was becoming more difficult by the day. He tried not to think about the things Connie had said to him. It only made him think about what it would be like not to be involved in his child's life. He still wasn't convinced he should be. He'd kept telling himself they'd be better off without him. Once the baby came, he would give the baby anything it needed. But he couldn't be involved in their lives any other way.

"It's what I've planned all long," he finally answered.

"How will you do that?

"You know," Morgan answered. "Medical expenses, clothes and things for the baby. Education expenses."

"But is that what you *want* to do?" Ernie asked, watching him closely.

"Of course," Morgan answered, but he couldn't meet his uncle's eyes.

"I get the feeling it isn't." Ernie took a seat behind his small desk, littered with memorabilia from his travels. "Why do you think that is?"

Morgan hated it when his uncle started asking questions like this. It reminded him of his mother, who could nail a person with guilt by doing nothing more than raising one eyebrow. "Because I still love her," he admitted.

"Ding, ding, ding. Give the sheriff the prize."

Morgan stared at his uncle, but saw no humor in his eyes. "All right," he said, throwing up his hands and dropping to a nearby chair, "I give up. What do you want me to do?"

"What I want isn't important," Ernie answered. "What is important is what *you* want—and I mean really want—and what Trish wants. The only way I see that you can get to that point is by being honest, both with yourself and with her. So in as few words as possible, tell her that what happened in Miami and what happened here in Desperation with John is what led you to cancel the wedding."

Morgan considered it for a brief second, and then shook his head. "I can't."

Ernie shook his head, too, as he got to his feet. "Then I guess we're done here." He reached his hand across the desk, and Morgan took it. "I wish I could do more, but good luck."

After thanking him, Morgan walked out the door. Taking Ernie's advice was the worst thing he could do. There was no reason to scare Trish with the past, when what he was trying to do was make sure her future was peaceful and without worry. Hers *and* the baby's.

No matter what he did, Trish was his every reason. When he'd canceled the wedding, it was to save her from the risk of leaving her a widow. When she'd said she would raise the baby without him, he was relieved and had offered financial support. It was the only thing to do that would assure her a life without constant worry. He'd seen that with Connie, long before Ben had been killed.

But could he remain on the outside looking in, as he'd planned, missing all the joys of being a real father?

He thought of all these things later, as he lay in bed, unable to sleep as conversations and images tumbled through his mind. No matter what he did, it wouldn't be the best thing. None of his options were. After he finally fell asleep, he dreamed of the wedding that wasn't.

Saturday morning dawned bright and cold. After calling Stu to let him know he'd be late, he drove to the Clayborne farm. Now that Aggie knew about the baby, maybe he could get some help from her to convince

Trish that they needed to start making arrangements. Once that was done, he would step out of Trish's life.

"Good morning, Miss Aggie," he said, when Trish's aunt answered the kitchen door after he'd knocked.

"Same to you, Sheriff Rule," she answered. "Trish is at Kate's if that's who you're looking for."

"No, I wasn't looking for Trish."

"Then what is it I can do for you this fine winter morning, Sheriff?"

He tried for a smile but found it difficult. "This isn't an official visit, Miss Aggie. It's personal business."

"Ah," she said, and then nodded. Holding the door open, she waved him inside. "Come on in, then."

He'd been inside the Clayborne kitchen hundreds of times, but this time he felt uncomfortable in the usually cozy surroundings.

"Go on, take a load off," Aggie said, indicating a chair with a nod. "Coffee?"

He cleared his throat as he slipped off his hat and shrugged out of his jacket. "Don't mind if I do, thanks."

After she'd poured him a cup, she brought it to the table and set it in front of him, then lowered herself to her chair. "This is about Trish, I take it."

"Yes, ma'am." He wrapped his hands around the hot cup and hoped for the best. "You see, Miss Aggie, I understand this is a difficult time for Trish."

"Is it?" she asked. "Why do you think that, Morgan?"

"The new doctor explained it," he began. "She said changes in the body—hormones and things like that— could bring on some instability. With emotions. Like Trish's crying," he hurried to explain.

"Or maybe it's difficult because it was only a few months ago that you canceled the wedding."

"Well, I—" He didn't know how much Trish had told her, but he wanted her to know that he was more than willing to help. "I want to make it easier for her, raising the baby on her own."

"Trish will be fine. Don't you worry about that," Aggie said, picking up her cup to take a sip of coffee.

Morgan realized he should have been prepared for this. "I want to do what's right."

"As in financial support, but other than that, she and the baby are on their own?"

"Yes," he said, and then realized that wasn't right. Shaking his head, he corrected his answer. "No." Even that didn't seem right, but he plunged ahead. "If you'd help me make Trish see that I want to do this for her and the baby, that it's the right thing to do—"

"Is it?"

"Yes."

Aggie put the cup down and studied him from across the table. "For who?

"For Trish. For the baby," he answered, unsure what Aggie was getting at.

Leaning back in her chair, Aggie crossed her arms. "And what about you? Is this right for you?"

He hesitated for a moment, and then chased the doubts away. "Yeah, I'd say it's the right thing for me." At least that's how he saw it. Most of the time. "But Trish and the baby come first."

He waited for Aggie to say more, even ask more questions. When she didn't, a cloak of unease fell over him. "You have a lot of sway with Trish, Miss Aggie. If you'd only help her see that—"

"Morgan Rule, you're a good man, but there are a lot of things you don't know about women."

"I'm aware of that, Miss Aggie, but I'd venture to say the same can be said about most men." He had to try one more time. "So will you help me?"

Aggie's chair scraped on the floor when she moved it back. Getting to her feet, she looked at him. "No."

"But—"

"Trish knows Kate and I are here for her," she said, her voice quiet but strong. But it also held kindness, as did her blue eyes. "We'll help her with whatever she needs. We're Claybornes. We know how to be a family. Do you?"

"It was Trish's decision to raise the baby without me," he pointed out in his defense.

"And you agreed to it."

She had him on that. "It's the only thing I could do," he admitted. "There are...reasons."

He could tell by the look on her face that it wouldn't do to argue or try another tactic. Aggie was not willing to help. "If it's all right," he said, giving up, "I'll come by to see Trish this evening, after she gets back from Kate's."

"Suit yourself," Aggie said with a shrug. "But you're on your own where Trish is concerned."

Nodding, he stood. "Thanks for listening to me, at least."

Aggie walked him to the door and placed a hand on his arm. "You're a good man, Morgan, but sometimes we have to put ourselves in the other person's shoes to understand."

"Yes, ma'am." All he knew was that sometimes the shoes of that other person pinched.

"TRISH, MORGAN'S HERE."

Morgan stood in the Clayborne hallway with Aggie and waited for Trish to come downstairs. He'd given it a lot of thought, and if it came down to telling her about what happened in Miami, then he would. He'd even tell her about John, but he hoped he wouldn't have to. Miami was far away, but John was right here in Desperation, and Morgan didn't want her to worry. That was his job, not hers.

When he heard footsteps, he looked up to see her descending the staircase, her lips pulled down in a frown and her eyes puzzled. "Hello, Morgan."

"Trish," he said, without emotion. When she reached the bottom of the stairs, he glanced at Aggie. "Is there somewhere we can talk in private?"

"The living room," Aggie answered, "and I'll make sure no one bothers you."

Trish's eyes widened, but all she said was, "Thank you, Aunt Aggie."

Aggie turned for the kitchen, and Morgan followed Trish into the living room. The room was seldom used, but he and Dusty had shared many weekends watching football and baseball games, so he felt at home in it. He hoped Trish would, too. They both needed to feel comfortable and at ease with each other. But as Trish took a seat on the big overstuffed chair, she didn't look at all receptive.

"What's this about, Morgan?" she asked, as he chose the end of the sofa closest to her.

"It's time we make some decisions about the arrangements," he answered, hoping this time she wouldn't brush him off.

Her chin went up, reminding him of her sister. It

hadn't escaped him how much this pregnancy had changed Trish. He didn't think it was bad that she was more independent, but it was taking some getting used to.

"What if I'm not ready to talk about finances?" she asked. "There's plenty of time for that in the next few months. I don't see why you're in such a rush."

He'd expected her to say something similar and he'd decided that if telling her the reason he'd called off their wedding would help, he would. "Maybe you'll understand my position after I tell you about some things."

"Like what?"

He was going against everything he believed was right, but he'd started and would have to finish. "The real reason I canceled our wedding."

Trish's eyes widened for a moment, and then she settled back in the chair. "All right."

After wondering all day how to tell her about his experience as a police officer in Miami, he decided to keep it as brief as possible. "I never mentioned anything about my job in Miami," he began, the words difficult to form, "or my partner or his family. I never told anyone in Desperation, except Ernie."

Trish leaned forward. "Morgan, did something bad happen in Miami?"

He nodded. "My partner was shot in his front yard in a drive-by shooting, while his wife and I stood watching."

There, he'd said it. And he felt like he'd reopened a wound. Would it ever heal?

"Oh, my—" she whispered, her eyes wide. "Why didn't you tell me, Morgan?"

"Because it had nothing to do with you or Desperation,

except to bring me here. It was as if it had happened in another lifetime, except that I couldn't forget."

"No one else knows?"

He shook his head and dangled his clasped hands between his knees. "Only Ernie and only because he needed to know why I was here."

"Morgan, that's so…" She closed her eyes, and when she opened them again, he could see the tears glistening in her eyes. "Were you and your partner close?" she asked.

"He was like a big brother to me when I first joined the force He showed me the ropes, helped me hone my skills and made me a better cop."

"He was older than you?"

"A few years. He made me a part of his family. His wife, Connie, spent hours talking to me about what it was like to be the wife of a cop in a city where there was constant bloodshed of some kind."

"I'm sure it's brutal," she said, reaching out to put her hand on his. "What you went through—" She shook her head and sighed. "Most people couldn't have gone on."

"Connie and the kids needed somebody, so I stayed for six months," he explained, remembering the time as clearly as if it had happened a week ago.

"How old were their kids?"

"Ben Junior was eleven, and Tasha was eight."

"Did they— Where were they when the shooting happened?"

"Asleep in their beds," he answered. "It was late. We'd had one of our Saturday-night barbecues." He looked up and into her eyes. "Ben loved to grill, and Connie would tease him about not knowing how to cook, but he sure could grill a mean steak. Sometimes he'd smoke ribs, but that night, it was the steaks."

They were silent for a moment, until Trish asked, "Did you see the car coming?"

He shook his head, remembering it as if it was yesterday. "Connie was on the porch steps, and I was standing in the middle of the yard. We were joking about the watermelon-seed-spitting contest we'd had and how Connie had beat us all." He was seeing it again, as if he was there. The dark road lit only by a few streetlamps, the small gas light glowing in the front yard. A dog barked down the street, and he heard the faint sound of garbage cans being tipped over. "My back was to the street. Ben was telling Connie again that he was sure she'd cheated, but he never finished the sentence. None of us heard the car as it approached." He clenched his hands together, not realizing Trish's was still on his. "I should have seen it. Heard it. Something."

"No, Morgan, you can't think of it that way."

He glanced over at her. "I wish I didn't think of it at all sometimes. I don't remember if the car's headlights were on. Probably not. I've never been able to answer that question. But I remember the sound of several shots, and then Ben went down. Then the squeal of tires, and I pulled my gun and spun around and started shooting. I know I hit the car and shattered at least one window, but the car just kept going."

"Did they find out who did it?

Her voice was soft and caring, and he nodded. "Some kids. Gang. Ben had testified against some of their family members who had been put away for a long time."

"I can only imagine how awful it was for you. And for Connie."

Nodding, he forced out the words. "She's a strong woman, but losing Ben was almost more than she could handle. She'd told me so many times how hard it was being the wife of a cop, not knowing if this night or that night would be when she'd get a call that something had happened and Ben was in the hospital or wouldn't be coming home. She never expected it to happen right in front of her."

"It's stayed with you all these years, hasn't it?"

"Every second of it," he admitted.

"But it's different here in Desperation," she said, her voice quiet as she squeezed his hands. "We don't have gangs or kids shooting out of cars. It's a quiet town, and I don't understand how what you've told me has to do with canceling our wedding."

"It just does."

Her hand came off his when she leaned back. "What do you mean?"

He wanted to reach for her hand as she had reached for his, but he couldn't. Instead, he tried to explain to her the fears he had and how he wanted to keep her safe.

"I thought Desperation would be peaceful. Safe," he said, getting to his feet. "When I first asked you to marry me, I believed everything would be good. But I found out this town isn't any safer than any other, that bad things can happen."

"What are you talking about?" she asked, watching him.

"I can't tell you," he answered. "Not the specifics, but something happened that made me realize that you wouldn't be any safer than Connie was. If anything happened to me, you'd be left alone, as hurt and lonely as Connie was."

"What are you trying to say, Morgan?"

He'd come to the part where he had to make her understand. "All of this is why I canceled our wedding."

"But you made it sound like—"

"I did," he admitted, unable to look at her. "But your tour wasn't the reason. I couldn't risk leaving you a widow like Connie."

The silence in the room wrapped around him. He knew she had questions, but he wouldn't say any more than he had to.

She stood, but she didn't move toward him. Instead, she walked to the other side of the room before turning around to face him. "But that doesn't make sense, Morgan," she said. "That was several years ago. You were right in thinking it's peaceful here. The risk you're so worried about is gone."

But it wasn't. Still, he wouldn't tell her about John. And he knew now that he had to do right by her and the baby. Keeping his distance wouldn't work. He should have done it in the beginning when she told him she was pregnant.

"So getting married is the right thing to do," he finally said. "Our baby needs a family, and I'll watch after both of you and make sure nothing happens to either of you. Or to me." He looked at her, meeting her puzzled gaze. "It *is* the right thing, Trish. You know that."

Her head moved slowly from side to side. "I don't think so."

"You don't think so what?"

"No, I—" She started to sit again but didn't, and then she paced along the opposite side of the room.

"No, getting married is not the answer. I'll raise the baby on my own as I'd planned, with help from Kate and Aunt Aggie. I won't marry you, Morgan. Not now, anyway."

"What?" He couldn't believe he'd poured out his heart to her and told her something he'd long ago sworn he would never tell anyone. And this was the answer he got for it?

Turning, she met his gaze. "Maybe later, but not now."

"That's not right, Trish. I'm offering you marriage, a home for you and our baby. But you're turning it down?"

"I'm sorry, but that's what I have to do. That's what's best."

He stared at her, willing her to come to her senses, but his were now so scrambled, he didn't know what to say to make her understand.

"I need to know why," he said, wounded in a way that even John's pistol could never do.

SINKING TO THE CHAIR, Trish let out a long sigh. She'd known Morgan would be upset. She didn't blame him. If she'd made up her mind sooner, they wouldn't have come to this point. But if she'd done that, she probably would never have known what happened to change him. At least something good had come of this. She had the answer to the question that had been keeping her awake at night for months.

"I'm sorry, Morgan," she said. "I'm not saying I'll never marry you. Maybe down the road things will change."

"Down the road?" He shook his head and stuffed

his hands into his pockets. "I don't believe this is happening."

"I'm glad you told me about Miami," she admitted, even knowing it wouldn't help. "I knew something had happened, but you never share things like this with me. It's as if you don't think I can handle it." Like Morgan, she shook her head in confusion.

He stiffened and looked her square in the eye. "I didn't share it with anyone but Ernie, and even then only because I had to. It's not something you go around telling people."

"I understand. But you took it upon yourself not to tell me, yet you made a decision for me that would affect me for the rest of my life."

"I decided for *us*."

Why couldn't he see? What did she need to say to make him understand that she was a part of this and had every right to know things that affected her, no matter how long ago they happened?

"No, Morgan, you decided that canceling the wedding was the best thing for *you*."

Jerking his hands from his pockets, he took a step toward her. "That's not true. I couldn't risk something happening to me that would leave you alone. I didn't want you to go through something like that."

She studied his face. He was a good man, an honorable man, and she understood that he was only doing this for her. Or thought he was. "Shouldn't that be *my* decision?"

"Not necessarily."

She was ready to give up. He saw things his way, not from the view of others, at least not in his personal life.

"You don't trust me enough to let me choose what's best for me."

"That's not true, either!"

She wouldn't argue, but he needed to know how she felt, so there would be no question. "You didn't tell me any of this until now. Not one single thing, not even a hint as to why you'd left Miami and came to Desperation. It's as if I don't really know who you are. You let me think my book tour was the reason you called off the wedding. You lied about that."

She knew she'd hit the mark when the anger left his eyes and was replaced with remorse. "I couldn't deal with what happened to Ben," he explained. "Not then, not now. I'll always feel it was my fault that he died that night. It should have been me, not him. I didn't have a wife and children."

"That's not the way life works."

"I know that," he admitted, his sorrow evident in his eyes. "I wanted to make sure you wouldn't ever go through what Connie has gone through all these years."

"But that's for me to decide," she said as kindly as she could. She knew he was hurting, and the last thing she wanted to do was inflict more pain. But he had to understand how she felt about what he'd done and how it couldn't happen again, not if they wanted to have any kind of relationship in the future.

"I only had your safety and best interest at heart," he insisted.

Trish nodded and felt the sting of tears in her eyes. She wouldn't let him see. In the state he was in, he'd only see it as weakness. "I'm sure you were thinking of me, but that doesn't make it right. I'm sorry, Morgan, but that's something we need to work on before we go any further. I didn't realize it before, but I'm seeing things in a different way. Maybe it's the pregnancy. I don't know."

Morgan didn't seem convinced. "I've told you everything now. How Ben died, how I watched Connie suffer, how I came here to Desperation thinking it would be safe." He looked directly at her, uncharacteristically, his pain reflected in his eyes, his defeat in his slumped shoulders. "Believe me, Trish, if I hadn't thought that, I never would have asked you to marry me. And then when—when somebody pulled a gun on me last June, I realized Desperation wasn't safe, either, and I would never be able to promise that I would always be here for you."

Trish's heart ached for the man she had fallen in love with years before and still loved. But there were still issues that needed to be worked through before she would consider marrying him. She tried to be gentle in choosing the words she had to speak. "Yet you now think we should get married. It doesn't work that way for me, Morgan. I won't marry you out of necessity, because there's a baby on the way and you—and I—think he or she should have both a father and mother and be a part of a traditional family." She shook her head, thinking of what could be but might not. "No. Honor doesn't make it the right thing to do."

"It's all I *can* do."

"Then we'll give it time."

She knew the second his anger got the best of him. She'd refused his offer of marriage, at least for the time being. Morgan had pride, and he wouldn't accept that she wasn't ready, not the way things stood between them.

"We don't *have* time, Trish."

Knowing she could do nothing more, except to hurt him, she stood. "We have a lifetime, no matter how long or short that is. And until you can understand yourself and me, I think it would be best if we didn't see each other for a while. The more you insist, the more I'll back away." Stepping closer to him, she reached for his hand and held it between hers. "That isn't what I want, Morgan. Please believe that."

It was hard to let go of him, but she did and turned away. For several seconds, he didn't move, but she finally heard him walk toward the door, then heard it open and close behind him. Drained, she sank to the sofa, where she sat and prayed that someday he would be able to deal with his past and see that there were no guarantees in life.

She didn't know how long she'd been sitting there when she heard the door open. Looking up, she saw Kate. "Come on in," she said, gathering what energy she had left.

"Is everything okay?" Kate asked, crossing the room to sit on the sofa beside her. "I couldn't help but overhear some of that."

"I'm not sure it will ever be okay," Trish said, feeling more confused than ever. "Am I doing the right thing, Kate?"

Kate took her hand and squeezed it. "I wish I could tell you, but only you know the answer."

"But I don't. Nothing seems right. What keeps going

through my mind is that he's never said he loves me, not since…"

"Since John held that gun on him?"

Trish stared at her. "He never said—"

"He didn't have to. I think we both know who it was. But I'll never say a word to anyone." She made an X on her heart with her finger. "I swear."

Trish almost smiled at the familiar childhood pledge. "I don't think Morgan reported it," Trish said. "If he had, John would still be in jail now. I don't understand why he didn't."

"I think he believes he's helping John."

"He's not. John needs professional help, and Morgan isn't the one to give it."

"And maybe he'll still get it. Morgan can only let kindness take him so far, and he may realize that what John did has ramifications he hadn't thought of before. Such as the two of you."

Sighing, Trish leaned her head back against the sofa and closed her eyes. "It's almost as if he's waiting for it to happen again, only with a different outcome. As if that's his destiny or something."

"He does love you, Trish," Kate said softly. "He loves you so much he was willing to give you up to keep you safe."

Opening her eyes, she sat up. "It just doesn't make sense."

"Love never does. Give him time."

"I would," Trish said, "but I don't think it will change things."

Chapter Twelve

Morgan hadn't meant to slam the door when he finally made it home to the Commune, but he'd used enough force that Ernie poked his head out of the office door.

"It's late," Ernie said, the scowl on his face proving his disapproval.

"Yeah, I know," Morgan answered and continued to the stairs. All he wanted was a shower and sleep…if sleep would come.

"Maybe you should come in here."

Morgan shrugged, crossed the foyer and started up the stairs. "Don't know why."

"No? Let's try slamming the door, for starters."

"Let's try forgetting about it."

"Morgan."

His foot froze on the stair, and he blew out a *whoosh* of air. Maybe he should get this over with. If Ernie had something to say, he'd listen. He owed him that much. If Ernie hadn't helped him out six years ago, there was no telling where he'd be right now.

"All right." Descending the way he'd come, but in a much worse mood, he joined his uncle and followed him into the office, taking a seat, but not caring and not ready to discuss the day he'd had. He'd listen to what his uncle had to say, and then call it a night. It had been a day he hoped to soon forget.

"Stu called earlier looking for you," Ernie announced as he settled in his easy chair.

"He found me. I was running late, but I made it. I've been there all evening."

"And the rest of the day?"

Morgan refused to look his uncle in the eye. He didn't know if he even wanted to tell him he'd been slam-dunked in the marriage department. "Here and there. Working. Not working."

"Talked to Trish, did you?"

Shoving to his feet, Morgan stood. He'd thought he could do this, but he couldn't. "Not now, Ernie."

"Now's as good a time as any."

It irked the hell out of Morgan that his uncle seemed so unaffected, as if he had expected things to go bad. There Ernie sat, waiting to hear what happened, and Morgan couldn't think about it, much less share the experience.

"Bottom line, I took your advice and told her about Miami," he admitted. "All she could say was she was sorry, but that I'd lied when I led her to believe her tour was the reason I canceled the wedding."

"And that's not true?" Ernie asked, watching him closely.

Morgan ran a hand through his hair. "Well, yeah, but I did it to protect her. That's what she doesn't seem to understand. Well, that and why I now want to make an honest woman of her."

"Aha."

"Aha?"

"I understand where you're coming from, and there's

an answer to your problem. But first, you need to figure out what it is."

"I don't know what you're talking about," Morgan replied, more confused than he had been when he'd walked in.

A thoughtful expression crossed Ernie's face. "You were always a serious boy, and now you're a serious man, sometimes overstudying things."

"I have to be this way to do the job I do," Morgan pointed out.

"True. But you keep things close to yourself. The opposite of my dad."

Morgan remembered his childhood. "It was Grandpa who got me interested in law enforcement," he said, thinking aloud. "All those stories he told me."

Ernie nodded. "I heard the same ones growing up. So did your mom. And your grandmother, too. It was more immediate then. We heard the story right after it happened. I think that's why your mom married your dad. An accountant's life seemed pretty tame compared to the stories we heard."

Morgan looked up at him. "But she never said a word to me."

"She wouldn't. But there you have it. Two extremes. He couldn't talk enough about it and you keep it locked inside. There's a happy medium you're going to have to find, Morgan. Not enough to frighten Trish, but you can't keep her in the dark, either."

Morgan thought about it. Maybe Ernie had something. But it still wasn't the answer he needed. "And you think that's the problem?"

"Could be. I'm not the one going through this." Ernie

stood slowly and stretched. "You think about it. I'm going to bed."

"Yeah," Morgan said, wondering what it was he was missing that Ernie could see. *He* sure couldn't see it. "Yeah, I'll do that."

But even the next morning, after a fitful night of sleep and drifting in and out of disturbing dreams he didn't remember upon waking, he still didn't have an answer. Hettie noticed immediately at breakfast that he was in a sour mood.

"Goodness, Morgan, you're like a bear with a thorn in its paw."

"I feel like one," he said, without thinking.

Getting up, Hettie crossed the room and quietly closed the door to the dining room where only the two of them sat having a late breakfast. "Aggie told me you talked with Trish," she said as she returned to her seat.

"She would," Morgan grumbled.

For a moment she was silent. "There's just one question that needs answering," she finally said.

"What's that?"

"Do you love Trish?"

All he could do was stare at her. "Of course I do."

"Have you bothered to tell her that?"

He considered the question before answering. "Not in so many words, I guess, but I think wanting to keep her safe from harm is proof enough of that." Knowing Hettie would dig until she got to the truth, he continued. "And I *did* suggest we should get married."

He'd never seen her look more disapproving. What had he done wrong?

Sighing, she shook her head. "Morgan Rule, lately you've been proving you are more of a fool than I ever thought. If you can't find a way to convince Trish that you want to marry her because you love her, not just because you've fathered a child, she might very well cut you out of her life and the baby's, too."

He was trying to digest what she'd said as she folded her napkin, placed it on the table and left the room. He was back to square one.

He did love Trish. He wanted to marry her, always had. He wanted to be a real father, for them to be a real family, and he'd told her so. He'd even told her about Miami and enough about what had happened with John so she'd understand. And she'd refused him.

How was he supposed to convince her that he loved her when she'd insisted they keep to themselves for a while? And for how long?

Later that afternoon, even though he didn't know what he could say, he tried calling Trish, but Aggie answered the phone. "Now, Morgan," she said when he asked to speak to Trish, "you need to give her some time. Things will work out for the best."

"I need to talk to her, Miss Aggie."

"She's at Kate and Dusty's. Now isn't a good time."

Before he could say more, she'd hung up.

He wasn't sure if he could get through Kate to Trish if he tried calling, so he didn't. But by the next day, he decided he might be able to talk Kate into being his ally. It was far-fetched, he knew, but any chance was better than none.

Kate, however, was like a brick wall and had very little to say except to leave Trish alone until he came to his senses. Because he hadn't reached that point and didn't know where bad sense ended and good sense started in all of it, he chalked it up as another failure and managed to get through the rest of that day and the day after.

But when Wednesday rolled around and he saw Trish in town, it was clear she was avoiding him. She nearly sprinted to her car when she saw him as she left the Chick-a-Lick Café and he was headed there for lunch.

By late Friday, he was beside himself, more confused than ever. Somehow, he thought, sitting at the desk in the sheriff's office, the tiny baby jersey spread before him, he had to figure this out. He had to find that middle Ernie had talked about.

Pushing away from the desk, he stood and walked to the window that looked out over Desperation's Main Street. Out of the corner of his eye, he saw two figures, one an older man in his seventies, the other a woman about the same age. Vern and Esther. According to everyone in town, Esther had been chasing Vern for years. Literally.

Was that going to be him? Would he be chasing after Trish for years and years while she ran away, the way Esther did with Vern? He couldn't let that happen. He wouldn't let it come to that.

He remembered his conversation with Dusty, how Kate's husband had told him that keeping secrets from the Clayborne women could lead to trouble. Dusty had been right. If he'd been honest with Trish when they'd first met, if he'd told her about Miami, maybe things would be different.

And he remembered what Connie had said, how she was thankful for the years she and Ben had spent together.

He'd found love in Desperation, and he wasn't willing to give it up. He *would* talk to Trish. He would find a way to make her listen, one last time. And maybe as he did, he would begin to understand himself.

The vision of Dusty chasing Kate through town at the July Fourth celebration came to mind. Dusty had gone so far as to rope Kate to get her to listen. If that's what it took, or something like that, then that's what he'd do.

And in that instant, Morgan knew what needed to be done.

TRISH SAT at the table in Kate's kitchen, surrounded by honey oak cabinets and frilly white curtains at the windows, so unlike Kate it was almost laughable. But Kate looked right at home that Saturday as they waited for Aggie to join them for an early evening meal. Kate had fixed Dusty's favorite fried chicken and Trish had fixed the trimmings, feeling smug that everything had turned out perfectly. Aunt Aggie was expected at any moment, and the sun was moving toward the horizon.

"It'll work out," Kate said for the hundredth time in the past week. "Morgan isn't a fool. He's smart."

Sighing, Trish nodded, but she didn't feel as positive as her sister did. "I hope so. Maybe I shouldn't be trying to avoid him."

"It's exactly what you should be doing. Just be patient a little longer."

"That's easy for you to say," Trish answered as the phone rang.

Kate hurried to answer it. "Yes, she's right here." Handing the phone to Trish, she said, "It's Hettie."

"Hi, Hettie," Trish greeted her when she took the phone. "What's going on?"

"I called the farm, but Aggie said you were there at

Kate's. By the way, Aggie is on her way and should be there any minute."

"Oh, good, dinner's almost ready."

Hettie whispered a sigh. "Oh, dear. I was hoping you'd have a few minutes to run into town."

Disappointing Hettie was something she hated to do. "What for?"

"I need your opinion on the new drapes for my apartment," Hettie rushed on. "I was planning to go into the city and get them as soon as possible, but I wanted to see what you thought first."

"You were going tonight?"

"No, no. First thing, right after church in the morning," Hettie explained, "before the crowds get too big to shop without a problem. But if you're busy..."

Trish glanced at Kate, who was setting the table with the pottery she'd received as a wedding gift. "Well, I suppose I could," she said, shrugging when Kate turned to look at her.

"No, no, I don't want to take you away from the family, even for a few minutes."

"It's not a problem, Hettie," Trish answered, feeling bad to be thinking only of herself. Hettie had always gone out of her way to help the Claybornes without even being asked. She'd been like Trish and Kate's fairy godmother for as long as they could remember. "I can be there in a few minutes and back without missing much of anything here. Kate can hold things up for a little while."

"Dusty wouldn't be too pleased," Hettie pointed out.

Trish laughed. "He'll survive. But really, Hettie, Kate won't mind and neither would I."

"You're sure?" Hettie asked, hesitating. "I'd feel bad if I made everyone change their plans. We can do it another time. Don't you worry."

"Hang on for one second, Hettie." Trish placed her hand over the receiver so Hettie wouldn't hear. "Kate, can we delay dinner for a little bit? Hettie needs my help. It shouldn't take long."

Kate shrugged. "It makes no difference to me. The gravy isn't made yet, and everything else can be kept warm. We've done that enough times during wheat harvest."

"Thanks," Trish told her, then removed her hand. "Hettie, Kate said she can hold dinner. I'll be there as quickly as I can."

"Oh, Trish, that's so nice of you. I should have called earlier, but I got busy with other things and simply forgot. You're always such a dear girl."

Trish smiled. "I'm happy to help whenever I can. You know that."

"Then I'll see you in ten minutes or so?"

"I'll be there soon."

When she'd said goodbye and hung up, Kate nudged her. "You're always a sucker for Hettie."

"And you're not?" Trish asked, grabbing her purse from the chair where she'd left it.

"Well..."

"Right," Trish said, laughing, and started for the door. "I won't be gone long. Something about needing my opinion on drapes for her apartment that she absolutely must get tomorrow after church."

"That's Hettie. If you'll turn the oven on to warm on your way out, I'll put everything in it and you can be on your way."

Trish did as requested, and then opened the door to step outside before calling over her shoulder, "Tell Dusty I promise I won't be gone long enough that he'll have to worry about starving."

Kate laughed. "I'll do that. But I'm sure he'll waste away, no matter what."

"No doubt about it," Trish answered with a wave of her hand as she hurried to her car.

The early evening was cold, with a hint of a breeze, and she pulled her coat around her as she slid inside her car and started the engine. Out on the road, she took a long look at her surroundings, appreciating the beautiful countryside. Clouds from earlier in the day banked in the northeast, moving away, while the sun shined against them, creating dark silhouettes of the bare trees in the distance.

Even the bleakness of winter held its own beauty, she thought with a sigh as she turned off the dirt road and onto the highway to drive on toward town. Knowing Morgan would be on duty and probably busy at the office, she was certain she was safe from seeing him at the Commune.

She wasn't a cold-weather person and was glad when the motor had warmed enough to turn on the heater. At the crossroad of Main Street, she came to a stop at the stop sign, quickly looked both ways and then proceeded into the intersection.

Surprised by the *whoop whoop* of a siren, she glanced in her rearview mirror to see flashing red lights behind her. "What the—"

She was tempted to keep going. She wasn't in the mood to see or talk to Morgan, and she was sure it was him in the patrol car behind her. Why would he feel the need to stop her, when he had to know she wasn't ready to continue the discussion she had thought had ended—at least for a while—the previous weekend? She was obviously going to find out, whether she wanted to or not.

Once she reached the other side of Main Street, she pulled slowly to the side of the road and stopped her car. Turning off the engine was not an option. She didn't want him to think she was eager for a chat, but was ready to leave at any moment.

Rolling down the window in anticipation, she stared straight ahead and drummed her fingers on the steering wheel. How long would this take?

She felt him rather than saw him stop at her open window. "License and registration, please."

Giving a short but quiet *humph* under her breath, she reached for her purse, pulled out her driver's license and handed it to him without glancing at the window. "Was I speeding?" she asked, a note of sarcasm in her voice.

"Your registration?"

She heaved a loud, irritated sigh and started to reach toward her glove compartment for the required paper-work. What was his problem?

"Step out of the car, miss."

Freezing, her hand in midair, she gave an unladylike grunt, much like her aunt's. "Enough, Morgan. What do you want?"

The door opened and a rush of cold air greeted her. "Please step out of the car."

"This is ridiculous," she muttered as she pulled her coat around her and scooted out the door. "Did Hettie send you after me? Is that it?"

"Just doing my job, miss. Now if you'll just wait—"

"For what?" she demanded, turning to look at him. "I didn't do anything wrong."

His expression was as stoic and impassive as always, and his voice cool when he answered, "The law requires a driver to bring the vehicle to a complete stop at a stop sign."

Straightening her shoulders, she lifted her chin in defiance at the absurdity of the situation. "I did."

"No, miss, you didn't."

Planting her hands on her hips, she drew herself up as tall as she could. "I did!"

"No, miss, you didn't."

"You're wrong. I stopped. I made sure I did. You can't do this, so just go fight some crime somewhere or something."

"Please calm down, miss."

"No, I won't. Stop this insane whatever you're doing and let me get on my way." She was done dealing with this foolishness and moved to return to her car.

"I'm sorry, but you'll have to come with me."

When he gently took her arm, she pulled away. "You're kidding!"

It was only a beat or two of the heart later that he looked down, met her gaze and said, "I don't kid."

It was enough to calm her down and stop arguing. "All right. Where are we going?"

"Would you turn off your engine, please?"

Cars had begun to gather on the street, but she barely noticed as she stared up at him. "You want me to leave my car here?"

"It'll be perfectly safe."

The whole thing was unbelievable, but the more she resisted, the longer this would take. "Fine."

When she was done, he stepped back. "Follow me, please."

With a shrug of resignation, she followed him to the cruiser, where he opened the back door and waited. "You want me to get in there? In the back? And just where was it you said we were going?"

"To the station."

"For what reason?"

"You're under arrest."

She couldn't believe this was happening. "You've got to be kidding," she told him. But the look on his face told her he was serious and arguing wouldn't change anything. After sliding into the backseat of the cruiser, she leaned forward. "You are so going to regret this, Morgan Rule."

The ride to the station was short and silent. Trish noticed Morgan glance in the mirror at her more than once, but she sat quietly, arms folded, and said nothing, although she couldn't remember ever feeling so furious with anyone.

When they arrived at their destination, he opened the back door and escorted her into the building. Several cars had followed them, and the occupants were now getting out, obviously curious about what was happening. Stu sat at the desk, his feet propped on the top of it, and he immediately swung his legs down, a look of guilt on his usually friendly face. Morgan held out his hand, and his deputy placed a ring of keys in it.

A handful of people stepped inside the office, whispering to each other, but Morgan didn't seem to notice. "This way," he said and led her to the lone cell.

Trish was incensed. "In *there?*"

"As I stated earlier, you're under arrest." He swung the cell door open and waited while she stepped inside.

"For what?" she asked, turning to face him.

He entered the small cell. "Failure to yield," he said and closed himself inside it with her.

"FAILURE TO YIELD?" Trish asked.

Morgan pretended not to hear. "Stu?"

"Yessir," his deputy said, jumping to his feet.

Morgan tossed the ring of keys to him. "You know what to do with them."

"Yessir."

Morgan watched as Stu pocketed the keys, grabbed his hat and left the station.

"Get him back here," Trish demanded, as more people entered the office to join the others.

Morgan ignored the growing audience and lowered himself to the lone cot and settled onto it. "Can't."

"Of course you can!"

"He'll be back when I tell him it's time."

"Well, it's time," she replied, her mouth pulled down in the deepest frown he'd ever seen on her face.

He suddenly wondered if he'd ever see her famous dimples again. If this plan of his didn't work, he was cooked. "I have some things I need to say to you," he told her as she stood watching him. When she started to reply, he held up his hand to silence her before she got going. "I know you didn't want to rehash all this again, but there are some things I have to tell you, and I can promise you that you won't be leaving until you hear them."

"That isn't likely," she said, turning her back to him.

"Suit yourself, Trish. But Stu won't be back with the keys until I tell him."

"You tell her, Sheriff!" someone shouted.

Even from behind, he saw her stiffen as she stood in the middle of the cell, silent.

Minutes ticked by slowly, and he finally clasped his hands behind his head and leaned back against the wall with a sigh. He had nothing better to do. Either this would end it for them, ruining his chances to ever be a real father to his child, or it would be a new beginning for them. At least that's what he hoped for as he sat there, his eyes closed. "Would you like to sit down?" he asked, opening his eyes to look at her.

She hesitated as she glanced back at him. "I might as well," she finally said.

She sat delicately on the other end of the cot, presented him with her back and said nothing.

"Now they're getting somewhere," a woman in the crowd said. Fifteen minutes passed before there was even a creak from the cot. She leaned sideways against the wall, pulling her knees up beneath her. He knew she couldn't be comfortable, but he wouldn't do anything to help. Not until she was ready to listen to him.

Outside the cell, people were getting restless. Morgan knew he could send them on their way, but he hoped they wouldn't get out of hand before Trish came to her senses and listened to him. When it was time to tell them to go, he would.

She moved slowly and stretched out her arms and legs. Sitting on the edge of the cot, she looked up and toward the office crowded with people. The fight appeared to have drained from her; she gave him a sideways glance. "My family is probably worried to death. You know that don't you?"

She obviously hadn't seen them in the crowd. "They're aware of the situation."

One blond eyebrow, only a shade darker than her pale hair, lifted. "Then I'm surprised Kate hasn't shown up with her shotgun."

He wouldn't have smiled if he hadn't seen the glint of humor in her eyes as she turned to look at him. "I guess she figured it was going to come to something like this. After all, this is Dusty's fault."

"Really," she said. "And how is that?"

"Oh, it was perfectly innocent," Morgan explained, stretching his own limbs. "He reminded me the other day about the Fourth of July celebration."

For a moment, she didn't appear to understand, and then she closed her eyes. "The lasso."

He nodded.

Another few seconds of silence passed, and then she turned to look at him. "All right. You win this one. Say whatever it is you have to say. This cot is too uncomfortable to stay on for much longer." Moving, she sighed. "And I'm hungry."

His moment of judgment was upon him, and he suddenly didn't know where to start. And then he thought of Hettie asking him if he'd told Trish he loved her. He knew where to start.

He cleared his throat and silently prayed this was the right thing to do. "Before I say more," he began, his voice thick with emotion, "the first thing I want to tell you is that I love you." As the crowd outside the cell quieted, he focused on Trish. "I've never stopped loving you since the day I pulled Kate over at the stop sign and ticketed her for not coming to a complete stop."

"She deserved it. She always slides through," she said without looking at him.

"I've noticed."

She glanced at him and smiled.

"You were right last Saturday when you said I lied when I canceled our wedding. I did, but it was done with the best of intentions."

"The road to hell—"

"Yeah, it is," he agreed before she could finish. "I vowed the night Ben was killed that I would never marry, never put a wife through what Connie went through. If nothing else, I'm a man of my word. I didn't count on meeting you in a small town in Oklahoma a year later. I tried not to love you, but I couldn't stop, and I thought it would be okay."

"I understand that."

"Can you hear what he's saying?" a woman in the crowd asked.

"Something about killing and never marrying," a man answered.

"Hush!" It was Aggie, and she didn't sound pleased. "Why don't you folks go home where you belong? This is family business, not Desperation."

"Sounds like desperation to me," another man replied.

"Go home, Gerald," Aggie told him.

Morgan waited while people began filing out of the office and left. When everyone was gone except the Claybornes, Ernie and Hettie, he dared a glance at Trish and kept his voice low. "There's more. Last June, John—" He hadn't meant to say the name.

She reached out and touched his hand. "I've already figured out who it was, Morgan," she said in a whisper. "I'll never breathe a word to anyone."

Nodding, he took a breath. "In my defense, I only let you think your tour was the reason for canceling the wedding because I wanted to shield you from what could happen. I should have told you about Ben in the beginning. I should have told you about John. That was wrong. I know that now."

She nodded, her face solemn and revealing nothing.

"There's more."

"All right."

"When you told me you were pregnant, I didn't know what to do. I'm an honorable man, Trish. Responsible. Marriage wasn't what I had in mind, not with what happened in the past, and I admit that I was relieved when you said you'd do it on your own. It's all been tearing me up. I wanted to keep you safe, and I believed that marriage would put you in harm's way. But I can't let you have the baby alone."

"It's been difficult, I'm sure."

"Worse than watching Ben die." His throat closed, and he had to force himself to continue. "But it wasn't that I didn't love you. In fact, that only made it harder."

Several seconds ticked by before she spoke. "None of us knows the future, Morgan. Not a lawman, not a teacher, not any of us. Anything can happen. Or not. We might live long, happy lives, we might not. But we make the best of the time we're given, without dwelling on what might or might not happen."

"I realize that now."

"If I had known, if you had told me about Ben and

John, I would have taken the risk, knowing whatever time we had together would be worth it, whether days, years or a lifetime."

"Yeah. I just never saw it that way. Not until yesterday. And now I understand that there are no guarantees. I need to grab happiness and hold on to it." He'd come to the end of what he had to say, but he wasn't finished. Not yet. "That's what I wanted to tell you tonight. Now I have something to ask."

Her movement was almost imperceptible, but he noticed that she moved away. "What's that?"

"What can I do to make things right?"

He watched her closely for signs of anything. Would she tell him he would have to step out of her life, their baby's life, and go on without what he expected would be his greatest joy? He held his breath as her eyes filled with tears.

"Oh, Morgan," she said, the tears spilling onto her cheeks.

When she covered her face with her hands, he moved without thinking and took them in his hands. "I need to know."

Taking a deep breath, she looked into his eyes. "I want to be your wife. I want us," she said, removing her hand from his to touch where their baby grew, "to be a family. A real family, not one where the husband immerses himself in his work, never sharing the ups and downs of the job or of life, but neither talking about them constantly. I want a partnership, where we help each other through the tough times and grow in both the good and bad ones."

He nodded, hoping, if given the chance, he could succeed. He knew only that he could try.

"What do you want?" she asked.

He didn't need to think to answer her. "I want to spend the rest of my life with you, however long that might be." But he wouldn't stop there. This was the time. "If you're willing to have me—risk and all—will you marry me?"

It was as if the sun had broken through a wall of dark clouds when she smiled. "I think I just might."

He ached with joy, but he wasn't finished. "And you'll help me when I fail to live up to the kind of husband and father I want to be?"

"I will."

"And you'll tell me if I'm keeping things to myself about something that's happened or not happened?"

"I will."

"And you'll marry me?"

Her face glowed with happiness. "I will."

He pulled her toward him, but she put up some resistance. "What?"

"Will you call Stu and tell him to let us out now?"

He tipped his head back and laughed. "I will." And then he pulled her into his arms and kissed her the way he'd wanted to from the very first time he'd met her, unrestrained, with a heart filled with love and no fear. They'd be a family, Trish, him and their baby. He'd be the best father he could be, with a little help from Trish. That's all he'd ever wanted, and now it was his. All it had taken was honesty. And love.

"I told you they'd get back together," Hettie. said.

"Did I ever say they wouldn't?" Aggie replied with an indignant sniff.

Kate sighed. "Oh, hush, you two. Isn't it wonderful?"

Morgan regretfully ended the kiss and turned to look at the three women. "Thanks for the vote of confidence, ladies. I should've known I could count on you." Holding Trish close, he glanced at the windows where the smiling faces of friends and neighbors were pressed to the glass as Ernie flashed them a thumb's-up. Morgan laughed again. "And that includes everyone in Desperation."

* * * * *

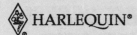

HARLEQUIN®

COMING NEXT MONTH

Available August 10, 2010

#1317 BABY BOMBSHELL
Babies & Bachelors USA
Lisa Ruff

#1318 DUSTY: WILD COWBOY
The Codys: The First Family of Rodeo
Cathy McDavid

#1319 THE MOMMY PROPOSAL
The Lone Star Dads Club
Cathy Gillen Thacker

#1320 HIS HIRED BABY
Safe Harbor Medical
Jacqueline Diamond

REQUEST YOUR FREE BOOKS!
2 FREE NOVELS PLUS 2 FREE GIFTS!

HARLEQUIN®

American ★ Romance®

Love, Home & Happiness!

YES! Please send me 2 FREE Harlequin® American Romance® novels and my 2 FREE gifts (gifts are worth about $10). After receiving them, if I don't wish to receive any more books, I can return the shipping statement marked "cancel." If I don't cancel, I will receive 4 brand-new novels every month and be billed just $4.24 per book in the U.S. or $4.99 per book in Canada. That's a saving of at least 15% off the cover price! It's quite a bargain! Shipping and handling is just 50¢ per book.* I understand that accepting the 2 free books and gifts places me under no obligation to buy anything. I can always return a shipment and cancel at any time. Even if I never buy another book from Harlequin, the two free books and gifts are mine to keep forever.

154/354 HDN E5LG

Name _____ (PLEASE PRINT)

Address _____ Apt. #

City _____ State/Prov. _____ Zip/Postal Code

Signature (if under 18, a parent or guardian must sign)

Mail to the **Harlequin Reader Service:**
IN U.S.A.: P.O. Box 1867, Buffalo, NY 14240-1867
IN CANADA: P.O. Box 609, Fort Erie, Ontario L2A 5X3

Not valid for current subscribers to Harlequin® American Romance® books.

Want to try two free books from another line?
Call 1-800-873-8635 or visit www.morefreebooks.com.

---

* Terms and prices subject to change without notice. Prices do not include applicable taxes. N.Y. residents add applicable sales tax. Canadian residents will be charged applicable provincial taxes and GST. Offer not valid in Quebec. This offer is limited to one order per household. All orders subject to approval. Credit or debit balances in a customer's account(s) may be offset by any other outstanding balance owed by or to the customer. Please allow 4 to 6 weeks for delivery. Offer available while quantities last.

Your Privacy: Harlequin is committed to protecting your privacy. Our Privacy Policy is available online at www.eHarlequin.com or upon request from the Reader Service. From time to time we make our lists of customers available to reputable third parties who may have a product or service of interest to you. If you would prefer we not share your name and address, please check here. ☐

Help us get it right—We strive for accurate, respectful and relevant communications. To clarify or modify your communication preferences, visit us at www.ReaderService.com/consumerschoice.

HAR10R

HARLEQUIN®

A *Romance*

FOR EVERY MOOD™

Spotlight on
Heart & Home

Heartwarming romances
where love can happen
right when you least expect it.

See the next page to enjoy a sneak peek
from Harlequin® American Romance®,
a Heart and Home series.

Five hunky Texas single fathers—five stories from
Cathy Gillen Thacker's LONE STAR DADS *miniseries.*
Here's an excerpt from the latest, THE MOMMY PROPOSAL
from Harlequin American Romance.

"I hear you work miracles," Nate Hutchinson drawled. Brooke Mitchell had just stepped into his lavishly appointed office in downtown Fort Worth, Texas.

"Sometimes, I do." Brooke smiled and took the sexy financier's hand in hers, shook it briefly.

"Good." Nate looked her straight in the eye. "Because I'm in need of a home makeover—fast. The son of an old friend is coming to live with me."

She was still tingling from the feel of his warm palm. "Temporarily or permanently?"

"If all goes according to plan, I'll adopt Landry by summer's end."

Brooke had heard the founder of Nate Hutchinson Financial Services was eligible, wealthy and generous to a fault. She hadn't known he was in the market for a family, but she supposed she shouldn't be surprised. But Brooke had figured a man as successful and handsome as Nate would want one the old-fashioned way. *Not that this was any of her business...*

"So what's the child like?" she asked crisply, trying not to think how the marine-blue of Nate's dress shirt deepened the hue of his eyes.

"I don't know." Nate took a seat behind his massive antique mahogany desk. He relaxed against the smooth leather of the chair. "I've never met him."

"Yet you've invited this kid to live with you permanently?"

"It's complicated. But I'm sure it's going to be fine."

Obviously Nate Hutchinson knew as little about teenage

boys as he did about decorating. But that wasn't her problem. Finding a way to do the assignment without getting the least bit emotionally involved was.

Find out how a young boy brings Nate and Brooke together in THE MOMMY PROPOSAL, coming August 2010 from Harlequin American Romance.